Eben Holden's Last Day A-Fishing

Also from Westphalia Press

westphaliapress.org

Eben Holding's
Last Day A-Fishing

by Irving Bacheller

WESTPHALIA PRESS
An imprint of Policy Studies Organization

Westphalia Press
An imprint of Policy Studies Organization
1527 New Hampshire Ave., NW
Washington, D.C. 20036
info@ipsonet.org

ISBN-13: 978-1-63391-142-0
ISBN-10: 163391142X

Cover design by Taillefer Long at Illuminated Stories:
www.illuminatedstories.com

Daniel Gutierrez-Sandoval, Executive Director
PSO and Westphalia Press

Rahima Schwenkbeck, Director of Media and Marketing
PSO and Westphalia Press

Updated material and comments on this edition
can be found at the Westphalia Press website:
www.westphaliapress.org

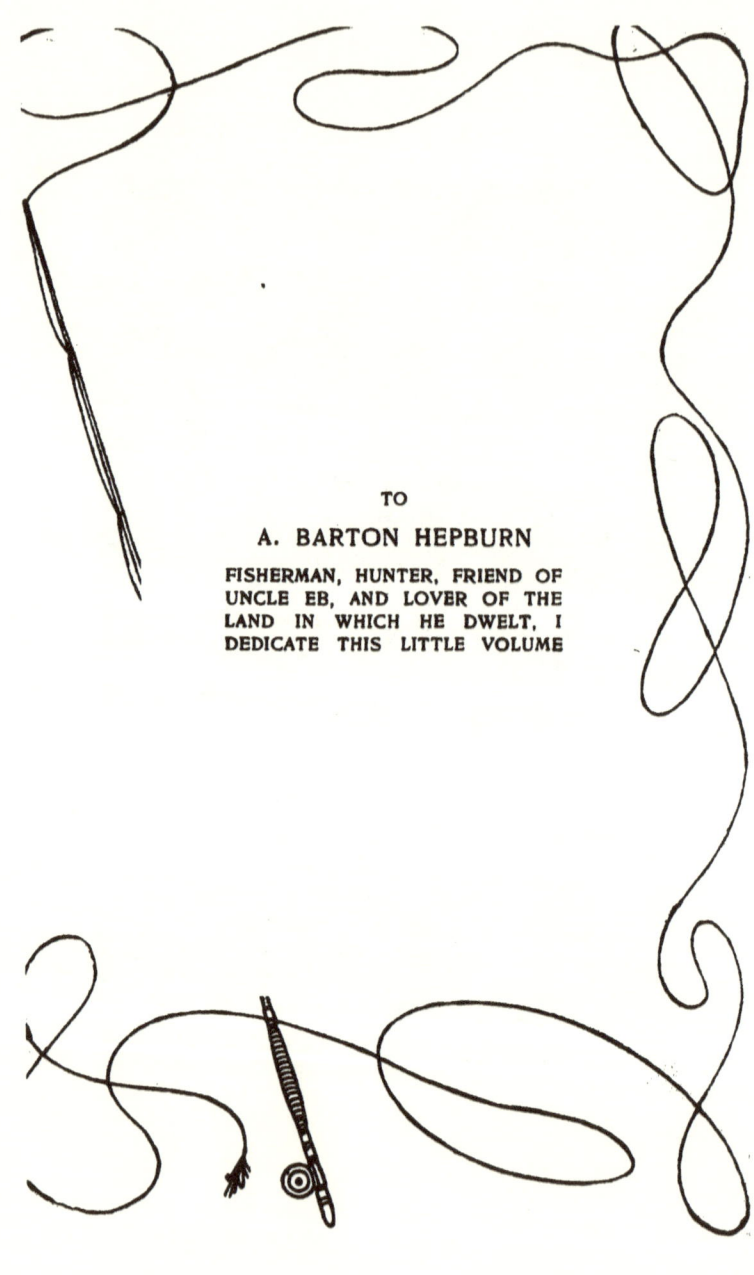

TO

A. BARTON HEPBURN

FISHERMAN, HUNTER, FRIEND OF
UNCLE EB, AND LOVER OF THE
LAND IN WHICH HE DWELT, I
DEDICATE THIS LITTLE VOLUME

EBEN HOLDEN'S
LAST DAY A-FISHING

BY
IRVING BACHELLER
AUTHOR OF
"EBEN HOLDEN" "SILAS STRONG"
ETC. ETC.

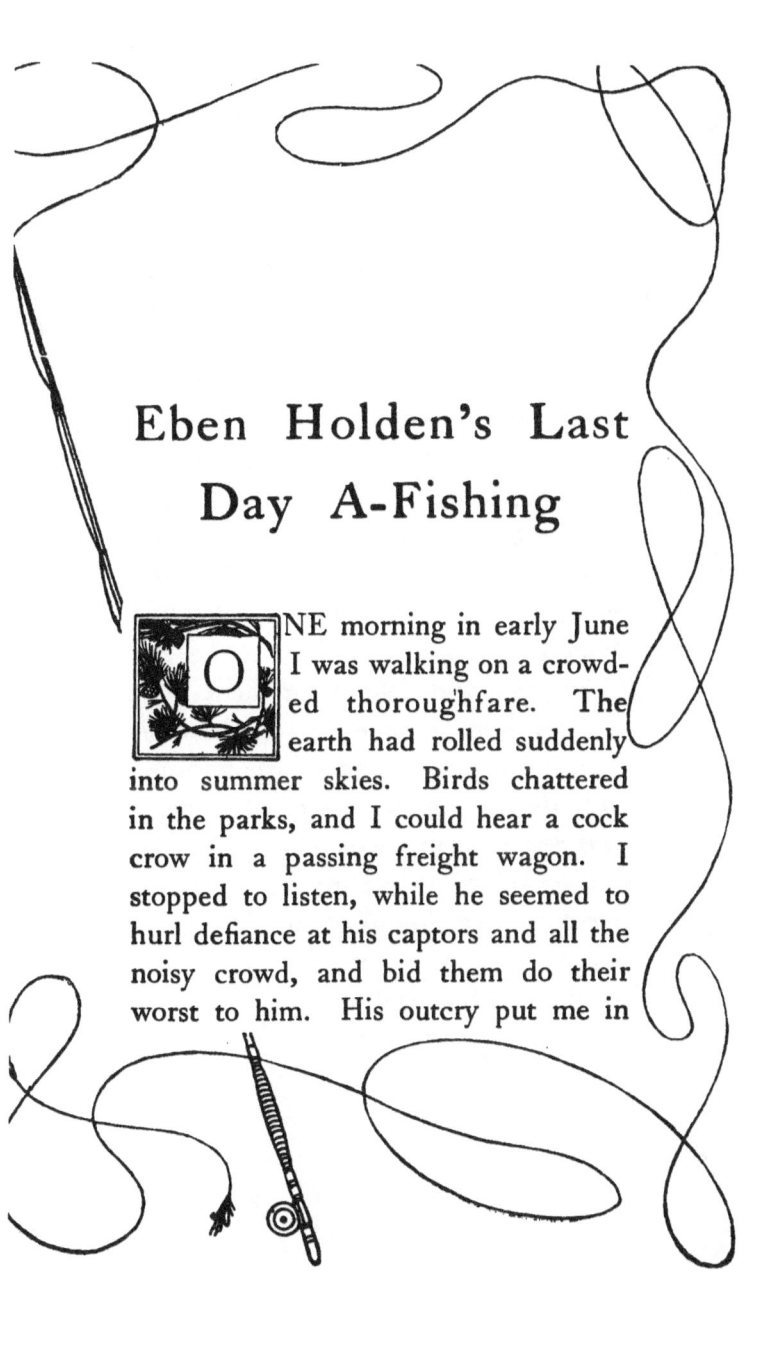

Eben Holden's Last
Day A-Fishing

ONE morning in early June I was walking on a crowded thoroughfare. The earth had rolled suddenly into summer skies. Birds chattered in the parks, and I could hear a cock crow in a passing freight wagon. I stopped to listen, while he seemed to hurl defiance at his captors and all the noisy crowd, and bid them do their worst to him. His outcry put me in

mind of my own imprisonment there
in the rock-bound city. As I thought
of it, I could see the green hills of the
North all starred with dandelions; I
could hear the full flow of the streams
that pass between them—you know—
and that evening we were on our way
to Hillsborough. Uncle Eb, then a
"likely boy" of eighty-six, and Elizabeth Brower and Lucinda Bisnette
were still in the old home. We had
quickly planned a holiday to be full
of surprise and delight for them.

They were in the midst of the days
that are few and silent—those adorned
with the fading flowers of old happiness and thoughts which are "the con-
clusion of the whole matter." As for
ourselves, we found them full of a
peace and charm I would fain impart
to those who read of them, if that

were possible. I know well how fee-
bly I shall do my task, but now, at last,
a time is come when it seems to call
me, and I can begin it with some hope
and courage. I shall try not to write
a book, nor a tale even, but mainly to
gather a few flowers, now full grown,
in the garden of remembrance. You
that see it growing lovelier in the
lengthening distance will understand
me.

Always, when our train went roaring
into the quiet village, we used to look
out of the car-window down across
the river and a smooth stretch of fields
into the edge of the little town. At a
small, familiar opening in the shade-
trees, almost half a mile from the
train, we never failed to see the flicker
of a white handkerchief. It signalled
their welcome. And then—well, I doubt

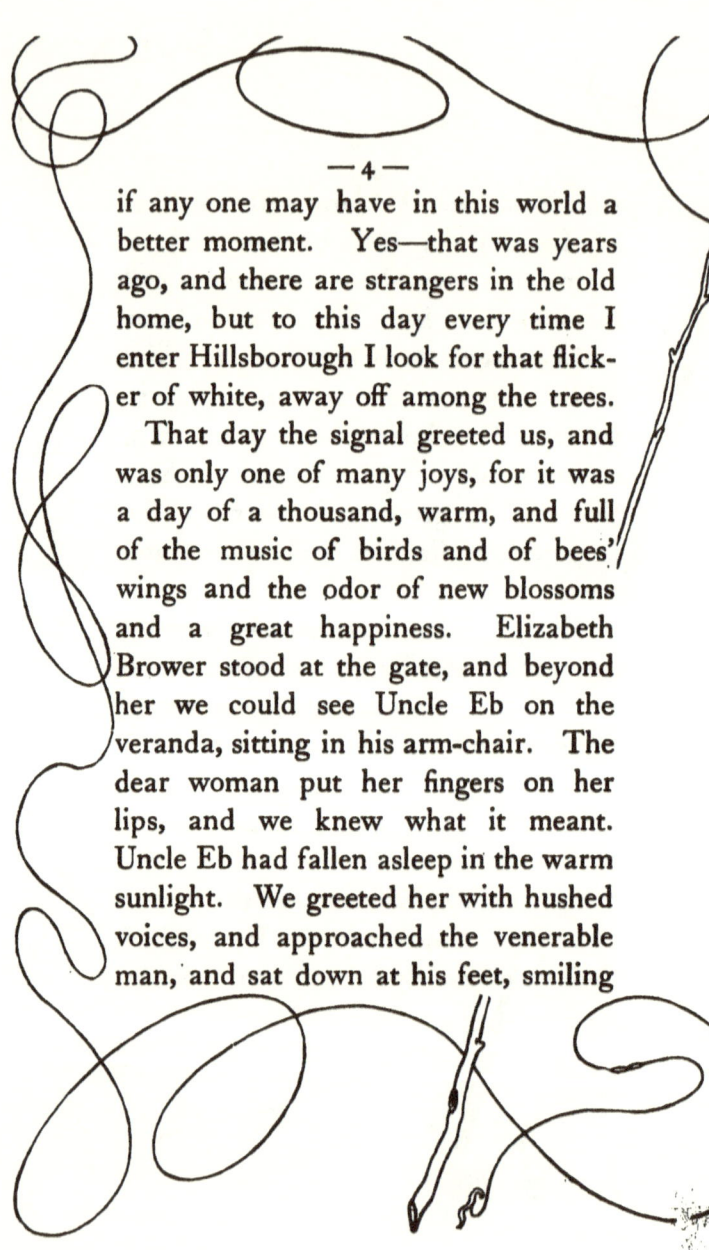

if any one may have in this world a better moment. Yes—that was years ago, and there are strangers in the old home, but to this day every time I enter Hillsborough I look for that flicker of white, away off among the trees.

That day the signal greeted us, and was only one of many joys, for it was a day of a thousand, warm, and full of the music of birds and of bees' wings and the odor of new blossoms and a great happiness. Elizabeth Brower stood at the gate, and beyond her we could see Uncle Eb on the veranda, sitting in his arm-chair. The dear woman put her fingers on her lips, and we knew what it meant. Uncle Eb had fallen asleep in the warm sunlight. We greeted her with hushed voices, and approached the venerable man, and sat down at his feet, smiling

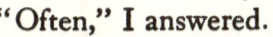

and looking up at his fine old face.
He continued to sleep, all unconscious
that we were near him. Soon we
heard him call in his dreams, just
above a whisper: "Here Fred! here
Fred!" It was the name of our old
dog, dead these many years. His nap
must have taken him far back—per-
haps into that long, westward journey
through woods and fields. I took his
hand in mine. He came out of his
dreams with a start, and looked up at
me.

"What!" said he. "Wal, I *declare.*"

He rose and clung to our hands and
looked into our faces with a full heart.

"A merry birthday!" I exclaimed.

"See here, Bill Brower," said he.
"You've hearn o' the joy o' Paradise?"

"Often," I answered.

"Wal, here's the key-note o' the song," said Uncle Eb. "Now look here, Liz Brower," he went on, "you tell 'Sindy we got to have the best dinner ever made by human hands. I'll bring some water."

Elizabeth, Uncle Eb, and that daughter of Grandma Bisnette were there.

Hope and her mother went into the sitting-room, and I followed them, while Uncle Eb went to the well for water. She looked up at us proudly as we stood before her, side by side.

"Turn around," she said, "an' let me look at ye careful."

She surveyed the fit and material of Hope's gown with great satisfaction.

"Look so ye was just goin' t' be married," she remarked.

We sat down presently upon the ancient hair-cloth sofa, with its knitted afghan of many colors lying folded against a curved arm. There were the old, plain, priceless things—the carpet, the pictures, a pyramid of plants and flowers in front of the large window, the centre-table, with its album and reading-lamp, the secretary and the what-not filled with books that were a part of our history.

There were the ingredients of that receipt which, as it were, had made the intellectual cake of my boyhood: Josephus' *History of the Jews* (the flour, two heaping volumes); *Ten Nights in a Bar-Room* (the milk and water, one volume); *Great Expectations*, *Bleak House*, and *David Copperfield* (the sugar, three volumes); *Pilgrim's Progress* (the egg, one volume); *Our Golden West* (the spice, one volume); *The Letters of Lord Chester-*

field (the frosting, one large table volume); Wrigglesworth's *Day of Doom* (the fire that did the baking).

Soon we found Uncle Eb with my boy David upon his knees on the veranda, and he was telling him the tale of *The Witch's Bridle*, which I had heard in my childhood, and we stood and listened. It was a relic of old Yankee folk-lore and immensely true.

"Once there was a young man who lived with his father an' mother in a little village," the story went. "An' there was a house in the village where a witch lived, an' it had a beautiful door. An' his mother told him that he must keep away from that house; but one night it looked so splendid that he opened the door an' went in, an' the witch spied him an' come and

looked into his face an' he thought she
was beautiful. An' she ast him to
put on her bridle, but he said no. An'
the ol' witch follered behind him as
careful as a cat after a bird, an' what
do ye s'pose she done?—waited until
he was sound asleep an' put her bridle
on him—that's what she done. Now,
ye see, when a witch puts her bridle on
any one it always turns him into a
hoss, an' a witch's hoss can go right
thro' the side of a house without makin'
a hole in it, an' can jump over trees an'
hills an' travel like the wind. She
rode him high an' low, an' brought him
back hum jest before daylight an'
took off the bridle an' that changed
him into a boy again. An' when he
woke up he was tired out an' all of a
tremble. An' ev'ry night the ol' witch
come for him an' put on her bridle an'

turned him into a hoss, an' rode him
all over the hills an' valleys until he
was about done fer, an' then fetched
him back, an' ev'ry morning when he
woke up he was a boy ag'in, an' was
lame an' sore an' had a headache an'
was sorry that he ever see the witch.
He grew poor an' spindlin', an' he'd
lay awake night after night to keep the
witch away. But o' course he had to
go to sleep some time, an' the minute
he forgot himself she'd slip in an' put
on the bridle an' away they'd go. An'
he grew poorer an' poorer an' less an'
less like a boy, an' more an' more like
an animal. By an' by, he got used to
bein' a hoss an' loved to go up in the
air an' hadn't any more heart in him
than my ol' mare.

"Wal, one night, what d'ye s'pose
happened? The witch come an' rode

him away, an' when she got back, by an' by, an' took off his bridle, he never changed a hair, but stayed a hoss. Why? 'Cause the boy in him was all wore out an' dead as a door-nail. Fact is, hosses can stan' more'n men. An' the witch grew sick o' him, an' said she wanted a better hoss, an' give him a cut an' turned him loose in the sky. An' ev'ry night fer years he galloped over the house-tops as if he was tryin' to find suthin, an' when I went to bed I used to hear him whinny way up in the dark, an' it sounded suthin' like this:"

Here he whinnied like the witch's horse, and went on:

"Keep on the ground, Dave, an' mind yer elders, 'cause a boy that has his own head is apt to get it caught in the witch's bridle. Same way with a

man, 'less he takes advice ev'ry day
from the great Father of all. They's
witches ev'rywhere, an' they're always
lookin' fer a hoss to ride."

"See here," said he, as soon as he
discovered us, "you must all come out
an' look at my garden."

"They want to rest," Elizabeth ob-
jected.

"No; we'd rather go with Uncle
Eb," said Hope, and we followed him
to the garden.

"Godfrey cordial! hear the birds!"
Uncle Eb went on, as we took the path
that crossed an edge of the clover
meadow. "Lot of 'em been gettin'
married, I guess. Don't do a thing
but sing an' laugh an' holler—like a
lot o' boys an' gals."

His strength had failed since we saw

him last. He was bent a little farther, his hands trembled, a small task affected his breathing, but he was the same cheerful, keen-minded man.

"Gardens are all right, but the sight of a hoe makes me shudder," said I.

"The hoe is a good teacher," he answered. "Man that don't hoe his character ev'ry few days won't have any."

"My wife hoes mine," I said.

"An' does it kind o' careless." He drew his hand over his mouth and cleared his throat and went on as if nothing had happened. "These things are a good deal like folks. Some grow up an' some grow down. I used to know a woman that looked like a turnip, and a gal that was like a flower, an' another that was like a pepper-plant, an' a man that was a reg'lar human onion."

"A garden always reminds me that it's about time to get your hook and line ready," I suggested.

He stopped and put his hand upon my arm. He glanced up at the sky, and seemed to note the direction of the wind.

"Say, by mighty!" he exclaimed. "You stop, or you'll make trouble."

"Think of Paradise Valley," I went on. "It will be green and sprinkled with blossoms, and the brook will be singing as it goes by."

"You quit!" he answered, with a little gesture of impatience. "Say!" he suggested, with enthusiasm, after a moment, "I wouldn't wonder but what the fish would bite—ye take it on the rapids there."

We returned to the house and he sat in his chair on the small veranda.

Robins were building their nest on a shelf near him, and were busy with their fetching and weaving.

"Look at the scalawags!" he laughed. "No, there ain't nothin' that's 'fraid o' me some way. I got a club one day an' tried to scare a mouse; but seems so she knew I was only foolin'. Now she's begun to bully me an' fetch her children right into my bedroom, an' I guess I'll have to git mad an' declare war."

I hailed a boy in the street, and sent him for a team, to be brought immediately after dinner.

When we sat down to eat, Uncle Eb put the same old question:

"Wal, how's ev'rything down there in the city?"

"About as usual."

"Too many folks there," he said,

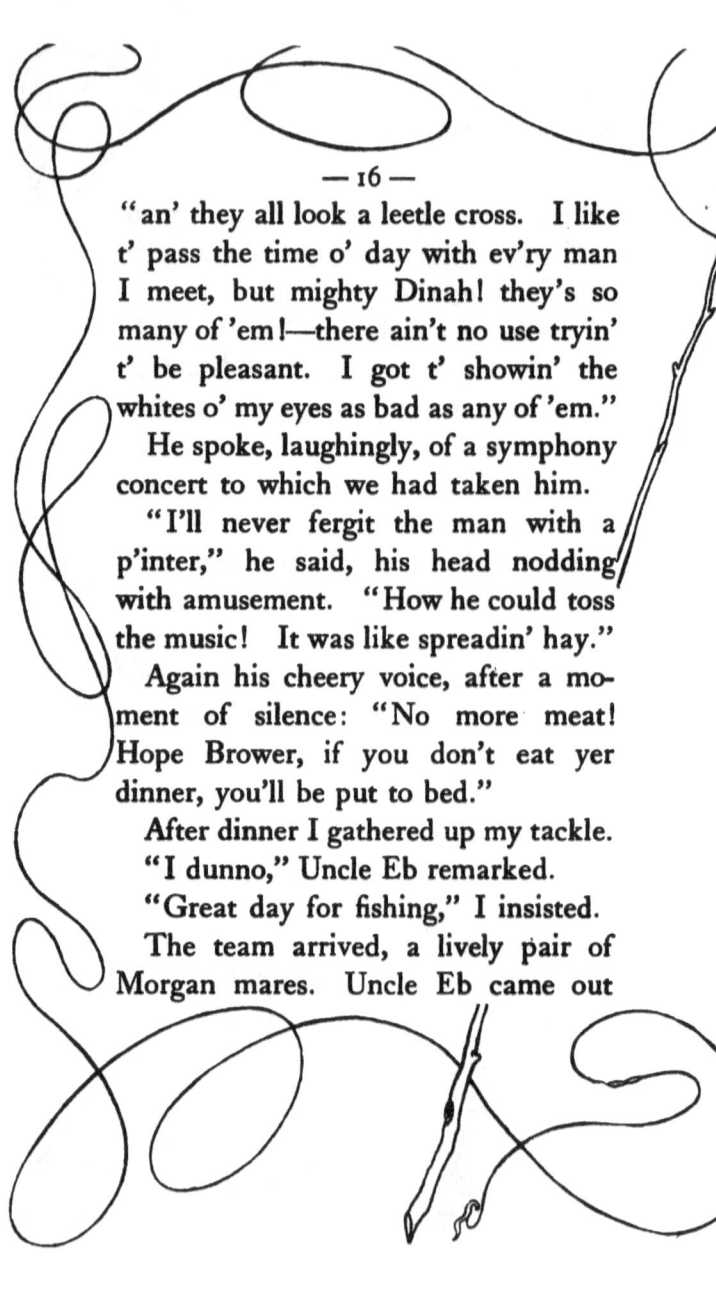

"an' they all look a leetle cross. I like t' pass the time o' day with ev'ry man I meet, but mighty Dinah! they's so many of 'em!—there ain't no use tryin' t' be pleasant. I got t' showin' the whites o' my eyes as bad as any of 'em."

He spoke, laughingly, of a symphony concert to which we had taken him.

"I'll never fergit the man with a p'inter," he said, his head nodding with amusement. "How he could toss the music! It was like spreadin' hay."

Again his cheery voice, after a moment of silence: "No more meat! Hope Brower, if you don't eat yer dinner, you'll be put to bed."

After dinner I gathered up my tackle.

"I dunno," Uncle Eb remarked.

"Great day for fishing," I insisted.

The team arrived, a lively pair of Morgan mares. Uncle Eb came out of the house in rubber boots, with his overcoat upon his arm.

"I'm 'fraid you better not go," said Elizabeth Brower from the door-step, with a look of anxiety, and now the trembling of his hands made me almost regret that I had tempted him.

"See here," said Uncle Eb, firmly, as he turned to my mother. "He's picked on me 'til I can't stan' it any longer. Ye couldn't keep me out o' that buggy with a gun."

I helped him in and took my place at his side, and away we went a pace of twelve miles to the hour, through town, across the flat, and up the stairway of the hills. We passed the old Hosper homestead.

"What's become of the deacon?" I asked.

"Dead; got sick o' life. Wouldn't

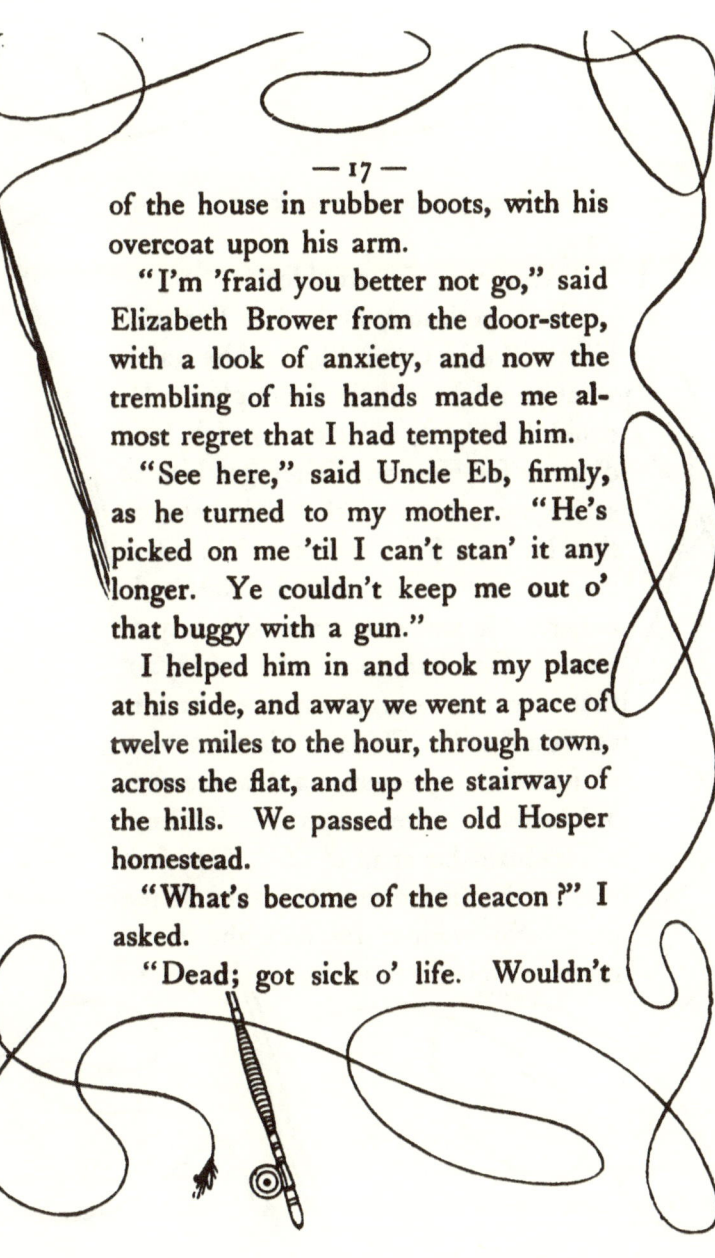

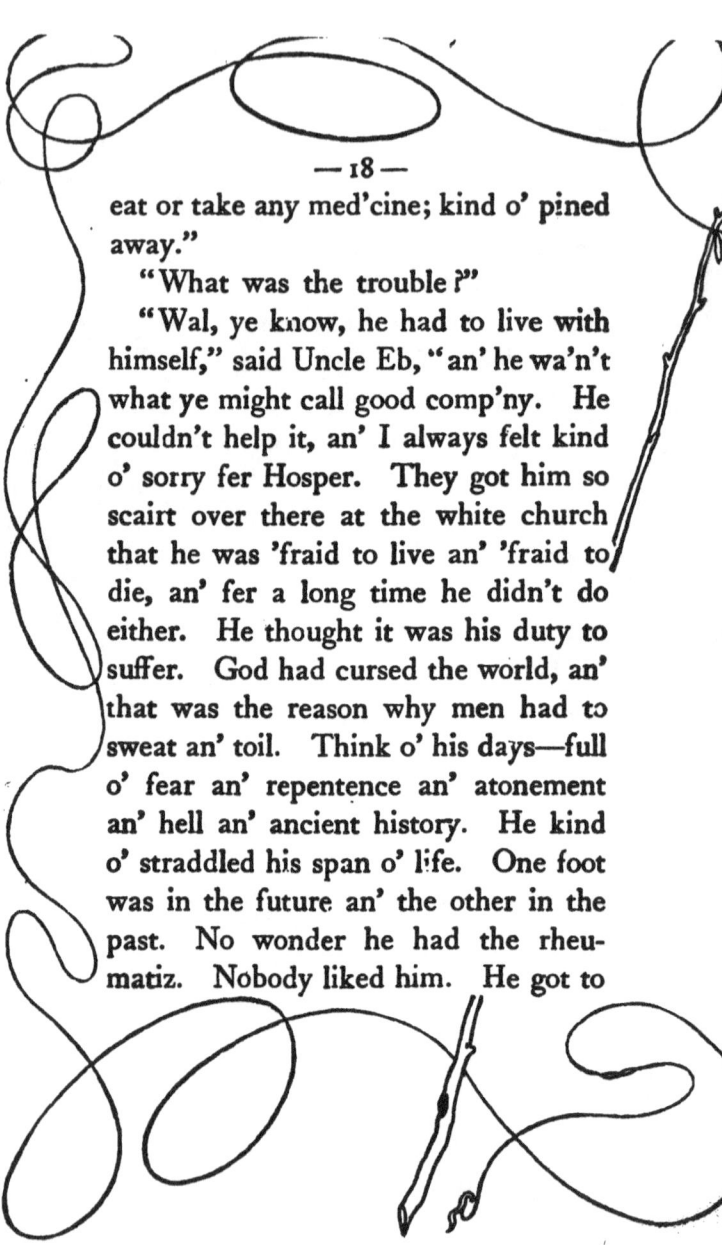

eat or take any med'cine; kind o' pined
away."

"What was the trouble?"

"Wal, ye know, he had to live with
himself," said Uncle Eb, "an' he wa'n't
what ye might call good comp'ny. He
couldn't help it, an' I always felt kind
o' sorry fer Hosper. They got him so
scairt over there at the white church
that he was 'fraid to live an' 'fraid to
die, an' fer a long time he didn't do
either. He thought it was his duty to
suffer. God had cursed the world, an'
that was the reason why men had to
sweat an' toil. Think o' his days—full
o' fear an' repentence an' atonement
an' hell an' ancient history. He kind
o' straddled his span o' life. One foot
was in the future an' the other in the
past. No wonder he had the rheumatiz. Nobody liked him. He got to

be a lonesome, sickly ol' man, I went
to see him one day. Says I:

"'Deacon, I wouldn't wonder if the
fish 'u'd bite.'

"'Fish!' says he, 'my mind ain't on
fish. I'm thinkin' o' my immortal
soul.'

"'Man's soul is like his stummick,'
says I. 'It ain't healthy 'less he can
fergit it. Come an' have some fun.'"

We rode in silence until Uncle Eb
went on:

"He seemed to think that God was a
kind of a bully, an' that he loved to
make men cowards. It don't seem
likely to me. I don't b'lieve He meant
toil fer a curse nuther. I couldn't be
happy 'less I had suthin' to do. Seems
's 'o' them who wrote down the plans
o' the Almighty made a mistake now
an' then, an' it ain't no wonder if they

did. No man can be perfect, special-
ly when he takes holt o' so big a job.
Prob'ly it was purty hot where they
lived, an' work didn't agree with 'em.
Now it looks to me as if that fust family
couldn't 'a' been very happy without
a thing to do. I don't wonder that
Cain an' Abel quarrelled. God must
'a' seen that the world lacked suthin'
very important. So He blessed it with
toil. I don't believe He ever intended
to curse it, 'cause, if He did, ye got to
own up that He ain't succeeded fust-
rate."

We came to the top of Bowman's
Hill and looked down into the little
valley, and were both silent.

"Time flies!" I remarked, presently.

"Beats all," Uncle Eb answered.

The Brower farm had run down, as
they say in the back country. The

house and stable were in ill repair.
Evil days had come to the neat and
cleanly fireside, where in the old time
Santa Claus had blessed us, and I had
heard the cry of the swift and felt the
touch of love and sorrow.

The tenant, a man who showed the
wear of hard times, put our team in
the stable.

"If you'd stayed here," said he,
with a glance at me, "this farm
wouldn't 'a' looked as it does now."

Uncle Eb smiled.

"No," said he; "the farm would 'a'
looked better, but he'd 'a' looked a
dum sight wuss."

He cleared his throat, and spoke of
the weather as if to soften the blow
a little.

I got my tackle ready while the man
dug worms for Uncle Eb—an angler

of the bait-and-sinker type. Soon we made our way slowly through the same old cow-path that wavered across the green slope now starred with soft, golden blossoms. It is curious, that conservatism of the cloven hoof, which, like water, follows its old path, having found the way of least resistance. In a few minutes we came near the rotted stump of Lone Pine.

"Hats off!" said Uncle Eb, as he uncovered.

In a second my hat was in my hand; for there, between our feet, was a lonely, half-forgotten grave—that of old Fred. Slowly, silently, we resumed our walk. My venerable friend was breathing hard. I supported him with my arm, and soon we sat down to rest upon a rock. The air was clear and still. There was not a cloud in the sky. A

hawk flew across the flat near us, his white butcher's apron stained with blood. He was flying low, with some small creature in his talons. It made me break the silence, and I said:

"There's a thing that puzzles me— the cruelty that is in all God's creation. It's a great slaughter-house, and every-thing that lives has the stain of blood upon it."

"It all teaches us that death ain't o' much account," said Uncle Eb. "It looks like cruelty, an' most of us think it a curse. Death is a wonderful bless-in'—that's the way it looks to me. Why, Bill Brower, ye've died twice al-ready. Fust the child, then the boy, an' each time ye wove a new body. Bym by yer loom is wore out. Got t' go git a new one. Ye'll begin t' feel as if yer body was a kind of a bad fit.

It'll be too small an' shabby an' un-comf'table.

"I 'member a boy over'n Vermont by the name o' Lem Barker. Grew so fast that the fust he knew his clo's begun to pinch him, an' the bottoms of his pants wouldn't 'sociate with his shoe-leather, an' his hands was way down below his coat sleeves, an' the old suit was wore so thin he didn't dast run er rassle fer fear it would bust an' drop off him. All he could do was to set an' think an' talk an' chaw ter-baccer an' walk as careful as a hen lookin' fer grasshoppers. He hadn't any confidence in that old suit, an' was kind o' 'fraid of it. One day he see a bear, an' it come nec'sary fer him to move quick, an' he split his clo's, an' hed to go hum in a rain-barrel. At fust he thought it was bad luck, but when his father got him a new suit he see that he was mistaken. We old folks are a good deal like poor Lem. We toddle around in our old clo's an' are a leetle bit afraid of 'em. It would be lucky for us if we could meet a bear. I'd like to go down to the brook there on the run jest as I used to. But I wouldn't dast try it. My body don't fit my spirit—that's what's the matter. Got to go an' have my measure took, an' throw 'way the old suit. An' I'll tell ye, Bill, I need a better outfit than what I've ever had—suthin'.stouter-wove an' han'somer an' more durable—suthin' fit fer a man. I'm goin' to hev it— call that a curse?"

He looked at his bony, trembling hands, and went on:

"It's all faded an' kind o' cold an' threadbare. My back couldn't carry

one small boy in a basket these days,
but I'd like t' carry all the boys in the
county, an' mebbe some time I'll have
a back broad 'nough. That'll be when
school's dismissed, an' I go off t' seek
my fortune, good deal as you did. I
'member how you went an' got some
new clo's there 'n New York fust thing.
An' they was splendid—better 'n any
ye could git in Hillsborough."

We heard footsteps in a moment, and
I turned and saw Jed Feary approaching us. He was past eighty years of
age, and his hair and beard were white,
and he walked slowly with a cane. He
stopped near us, and began to laugh as
we greeted him.

"Heard you was here," he said, "an'
Rans Walker druv me down the road."

"Stump ye t' rassle with me," said
Uncle Eb, with a smile.

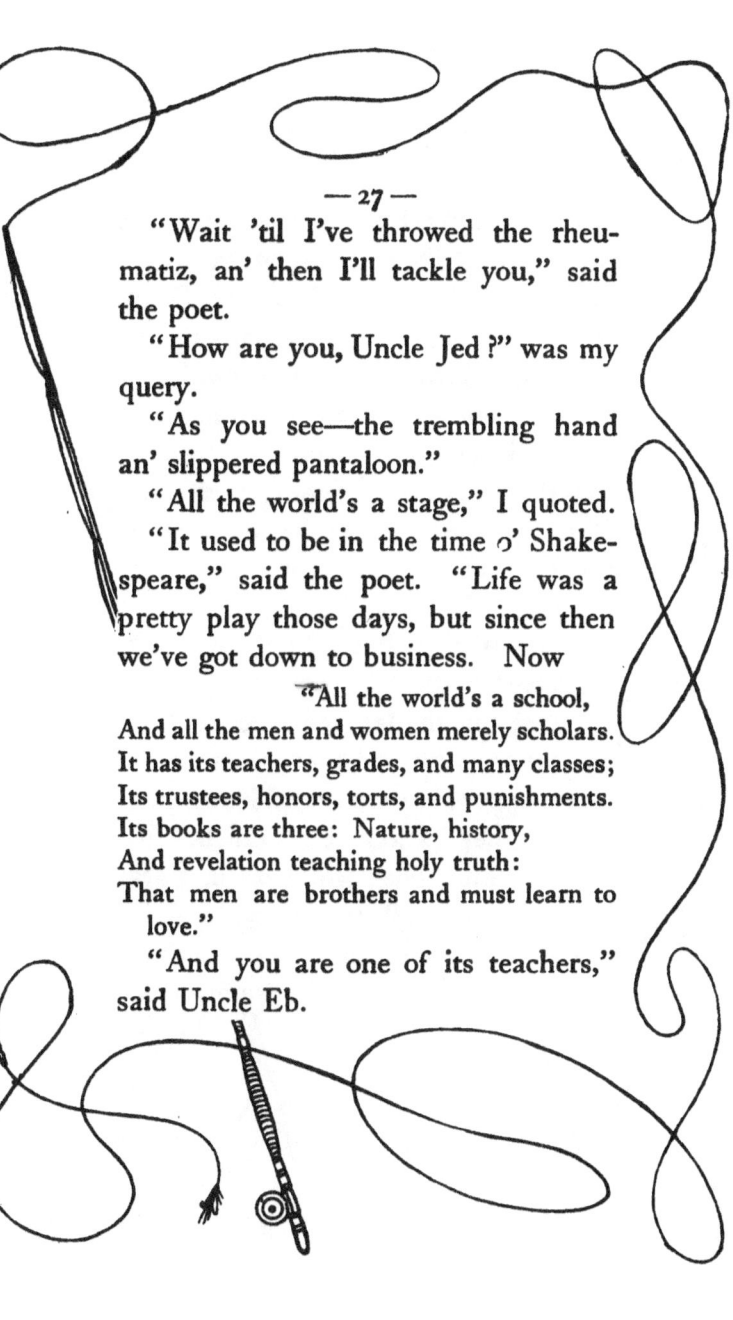

"Wait 'til I've throwed the rheumatiz, an' then I'll tackle you," said the poet.

"How are you, Uncle Jed ?" was my query.

"As you see—the trembling hand an' slippered pantaloon."

"All the world's a stage," I quoted.

"It used to be in the time o' Shakespeare," said the poet. "Life was a pretty play those days, but since then we've got down to business. Now

"All the world's a school,
And all the men and women merely scholars.
It has its teachers, grades, and many classes;
Its trustees, honors, torts, and punishments.
Its books are three: Nature, history,
And revelation teaching holy truth:
That men are brothers and must learn to
     love."

"And you are one of its teachers," said Uncle Eb.

"I'm only a humble student," said the poet. "Think what we've learnt in a hundred years. That little Devil, who rode across Europe killing an' burning an' spreading terror until they stopped him at Waterloo, he taught us a great lesson. He made us hate war, and that was the beginning o' the end of it. There were to be other wars, but they have been steps only in the conquest of Peace."

"And there will be no more war?" I queried.

"Yes; but the learned races will put an end to it by and by," he went on. "The upper classes have all learnt their lesson—they know too much. We know suthin' 'bout war here in Faraway. Let me tell ye a story."

The old poet sat on a rock near, and began this little epic of the countryside:

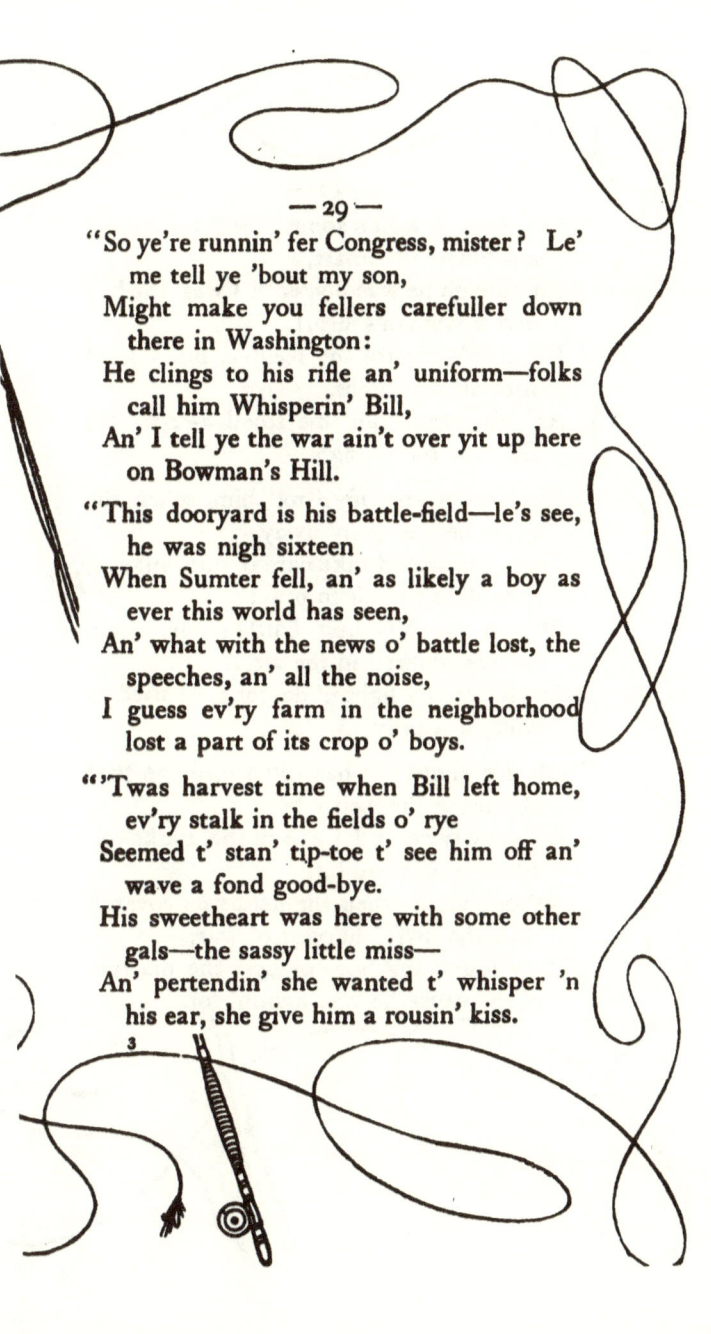

"So ye're runnin' fer Congress, mister? Le'
    me tell ye 'bout my son,
Might make you fellers carefuller down
    there in Washington:
He clings to his rifle an' uniform—folks
    call him Whisperin' Bill,
An' I tell ye the war ain't over yit up here
    on Bowman's Hill.

"This dooryard is his battle-field—le's see,
    he was nigh sixteen
When Sumter fell, an' as likely a boy as
    ever this world has seen,
An' what with the news o' battle lost, the
    speeches, an' all the noise,
I guess ev'ry farm in the neighborhood
    lost a part of its crop o' boys.

"'Twas harvest time when Bill left home,
    ev'ry stalk in the fields o' rye
Seemed t' stan' tip-toe t' see him off an'
    wave a fond good-bye.
His sweetheart was here with some other
    gals—the sassy little miss—
An' pertendin' she wanted t' whisper 'n
    his ear, she give him a rousin' kiss.

3

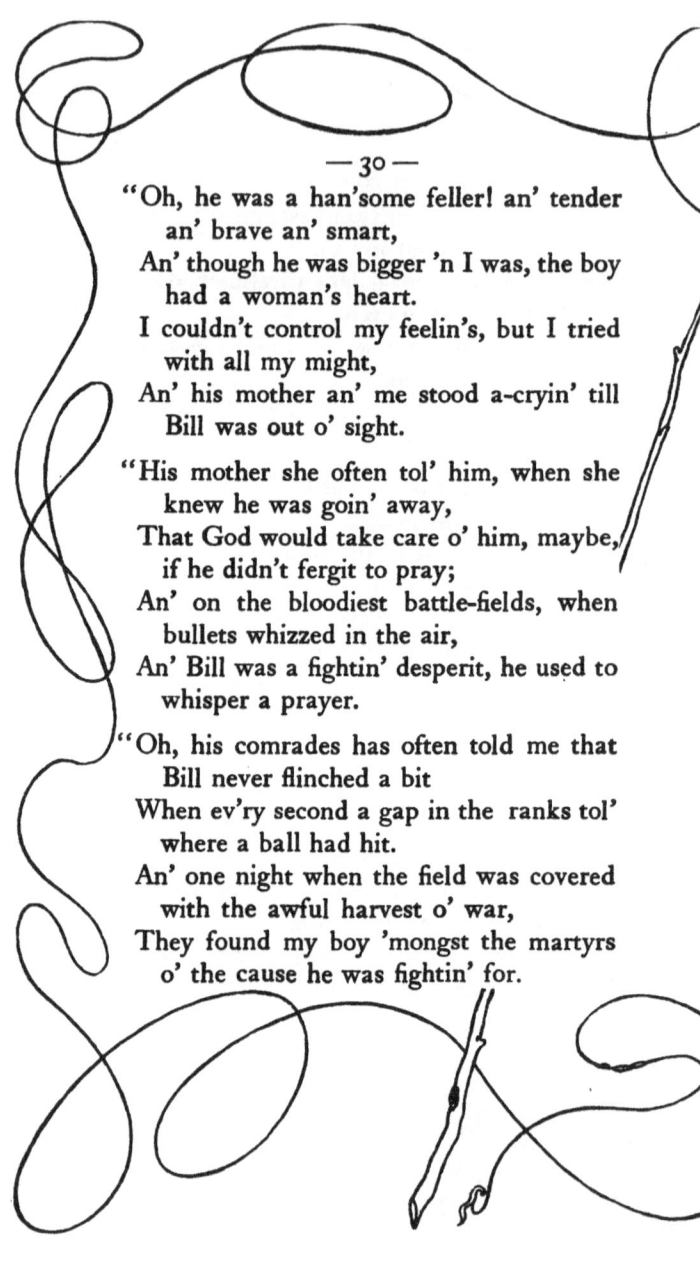

"Oh, he was a han'some feller! an' tender
    an' brave an' smart,
An' though he was bigger 'n I was, the boy
    had a woman's heart.
I couldn't control my feelin's, but I tried
    with all my might,
An' his mother an' me stood a-cryin' till
    Bill was out o' sight.

"His mother she often tol' him, when she
    knew he was goin' away,
That God would take care o' him, maybe,
    if he didn't fergit to pray;
An' on the bloodiest battle-fields, when
    bullets whizzed in the air,
An' Bill was a fightin' desperit, he used to
    whisper a prayer.

"Oh, his comrades has often told me that
    Bill never flinched a bit
When ev'ry second a gap in the ranks tol'
    where a ball had hit.
An' one night when the field was covered
    with the awful harvest o' war,
They found my boy 'mongst the martyrs
    o' the cause he was fightin' for.

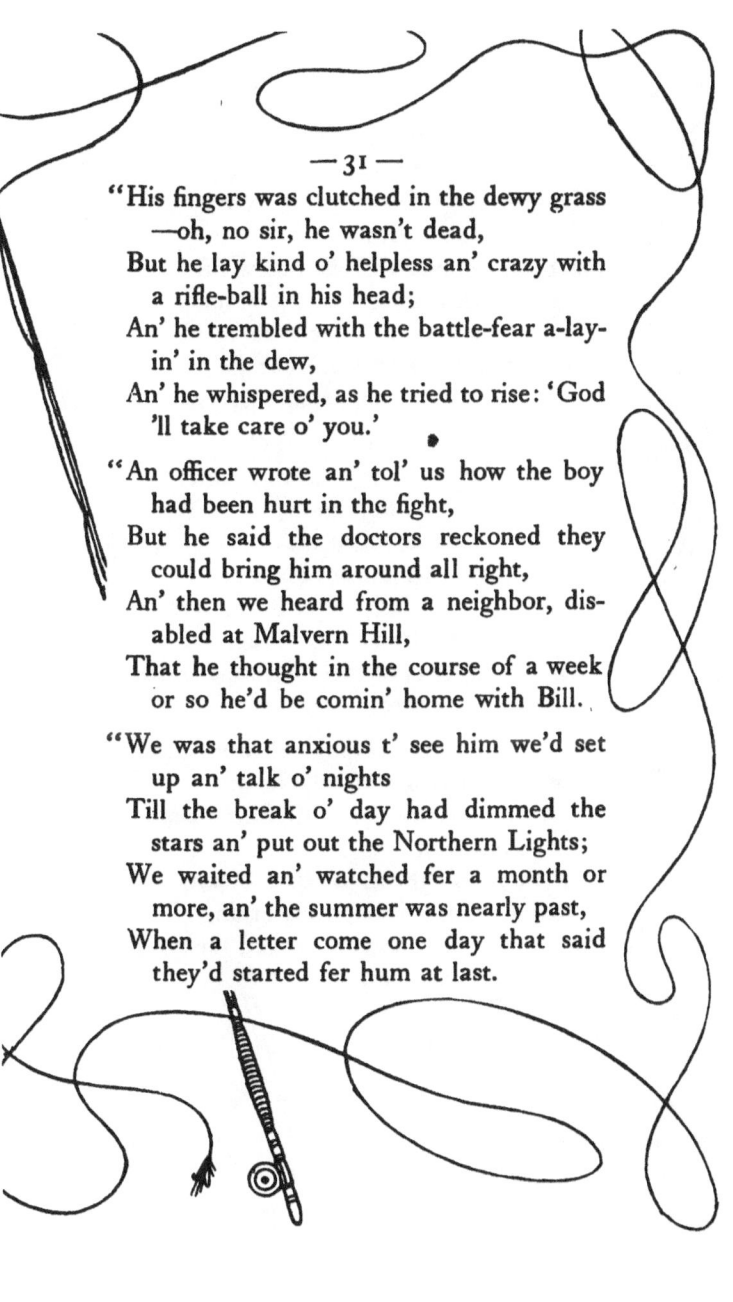

"His fingers was clutched in the dewy grass
   —oh, no sir, he wasn't dead,
But he lay kind o' helpless an' crazy with
   a rifle-ball in his head;
An' he trembled with the battle-fear a-lay-
   in' in the dew,
An' he whispered, as he tried to rise: 'God
   'll take care o' you.'

"An officer wrote an' tol' us how the boy
   had been hurt in the fight,
But he said the doctors reckoned they
   could bring him around all right,
An' then we heard from a neighbor, dis-
   abled at Malvern Hill,
That he thought in the course of a week
   or so he'd be comin' home with Bill.

"We was that anxious t' see him we'd set
   up an' talk o' nights
Till the break o' day had dimmed the
   stars an' put out the Northern Lights;
We waited an' watched fer a month or
   more, an' the summer was nearly past,
When a letter come one day that said
   they'd started fer hum at last.

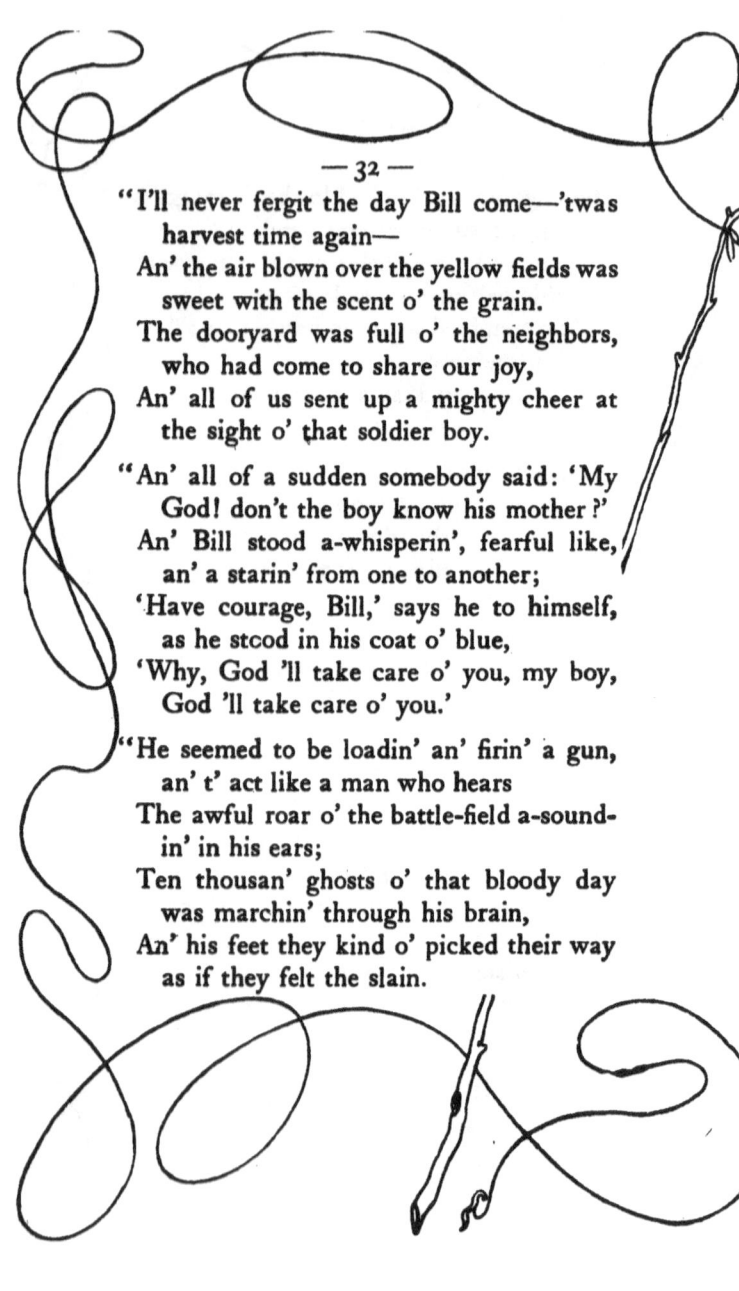

"I'll never fergit the day Bill come—'twas
    harvest time again—
An' the air blown over the yellow fields was
    sweet with the scent o' the grain.
The dooryard was full o' the neighbors,
    who had come to share our joy,
An' all of us sent up a mighty cheer at
    the sight o' that soldier boy.

"An' all of a sudden somebody said: 'My
    God! don't the boy know his mother?'
An' Bill stood a-whisperin', fearful like,
    an' a starin' from one to another;
'Have courage, Bill,' says he to himself,
    as he stood in his coat o' blue,
'Why, God 'll take care o' you, my boy,
    God 'll take care o' you.'

"He seemed to be loadin' an' firin' a gun,
    an' t' act like a man who hears
The awful roar o' the battle-field a-sound-
    in' in his ears;
Ten thousan' ghosts o' that bloody day
    was marchin' through his brain,
An' his feet they kind o' picked their way
    as if they felt the slain.

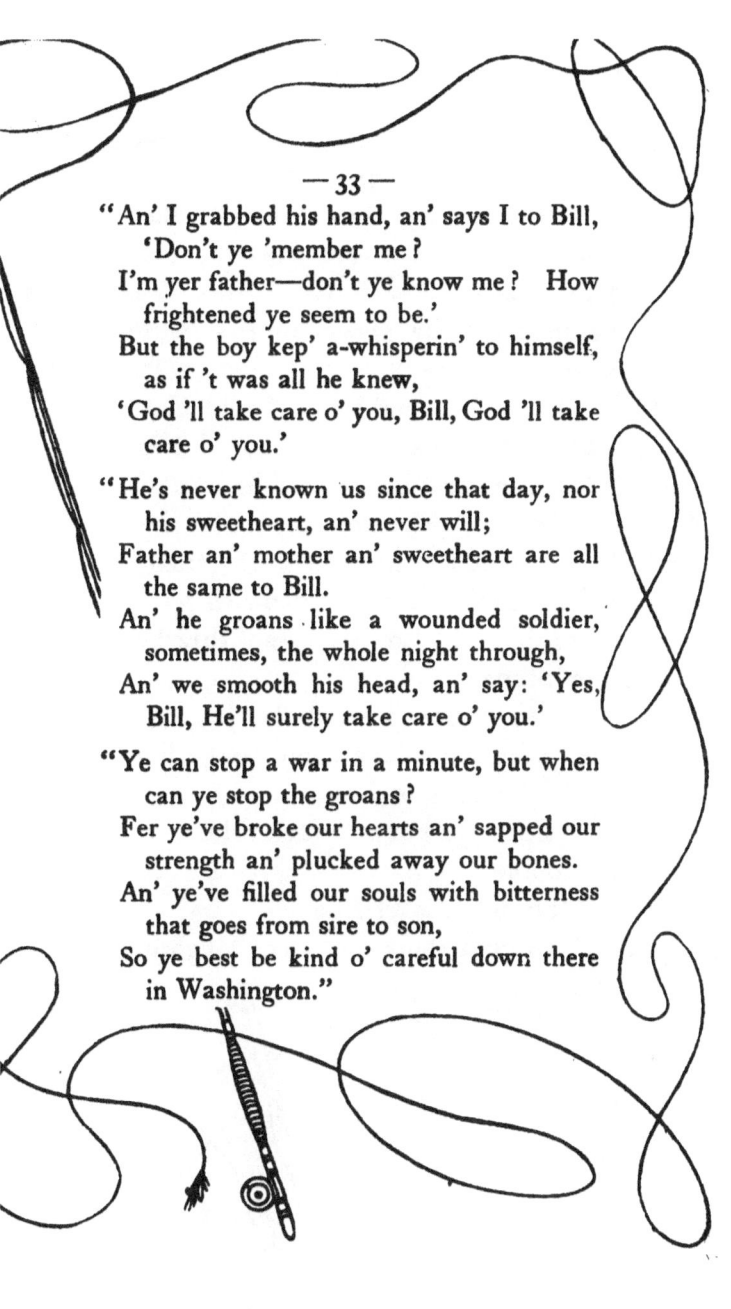

"An' I grabbed his hand, an' says I to Bill,
  'Don't ye 'member me?
I'm yer father—don't ye know me? How
  frightened ye seem to be.'
But the boy kep' a-whisperin' to himself,
  as if 't was all he knew,
'God 'll take care o' you, Bill, God 'll take
  care o' you.'

"He's never known us since that day, nor
  his sweetheart, an' never will;
Father an' mother an' sweetheart are all
  the same to Bill.
An' he groans like a wounded soldier,
  sometimes, the whole night through,
An' we smooth his head, an' say: 'Yes,
  Bill, He'll surely take care o' you.'

"Ye can stop a war in a minute, but when
  can ye stop the groans?
Fer ye've broke our hearts an' sapped our
  strength an' plucked away our bones.
An' ye've filled our souls with bitterness
  that goes from sire to son,
So ye best be kind o' careful down there
  in Washington."

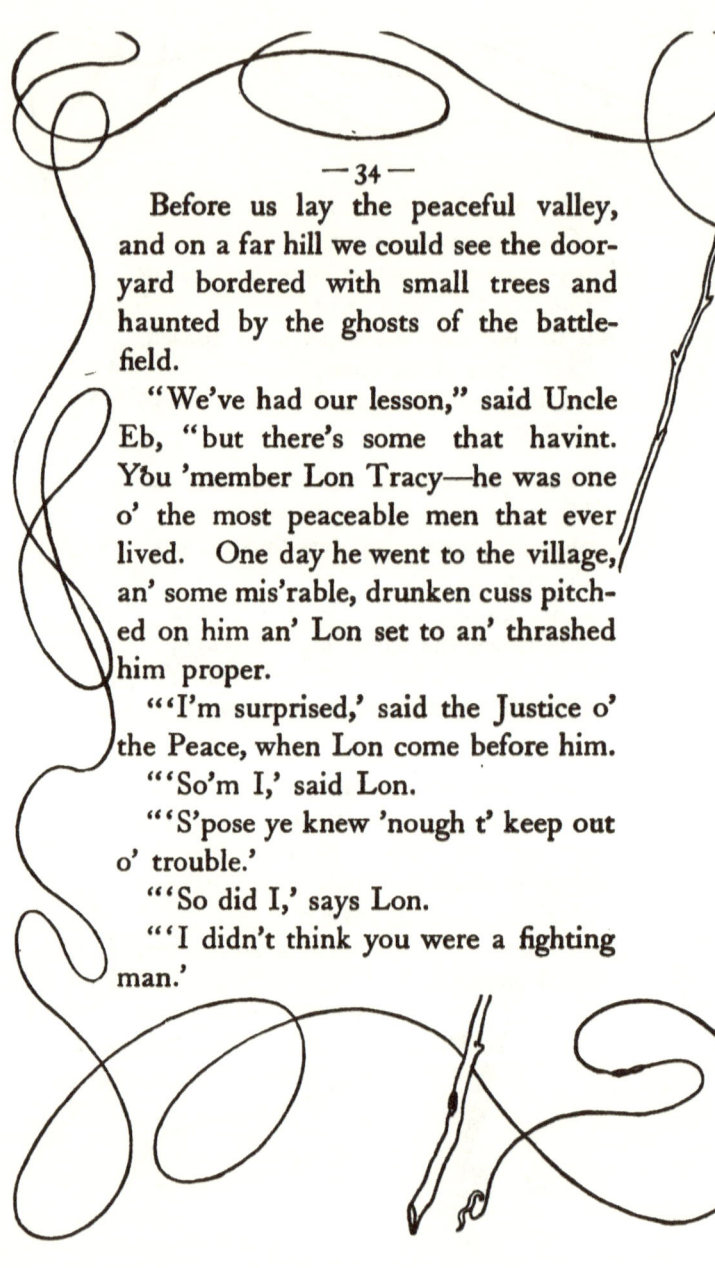

Before us lay the peaceful valley, and on a far hill we could see the dooryard bordered with small trees and haunted by the ghosts of the battlefield.

"We've had our lesson," said Uncle Eb, "but there's some that havint. You 'member Lon Tracy—he was one o' the most peaceable men that ever lived. One day he went to the village, an' some mis'rable, drunken cuss pitched on him an' Lon set to an' thrashed him proper.

"'I'm surprised,' said the Justice o' the Peace, when Lon come before him.

"'So'm I,' said Lon.

"'S'pose ye knew 'nough t' keep out o' trouble.'

"'So did I,' says Lon.

"'I didn't think you were a fighting man.'

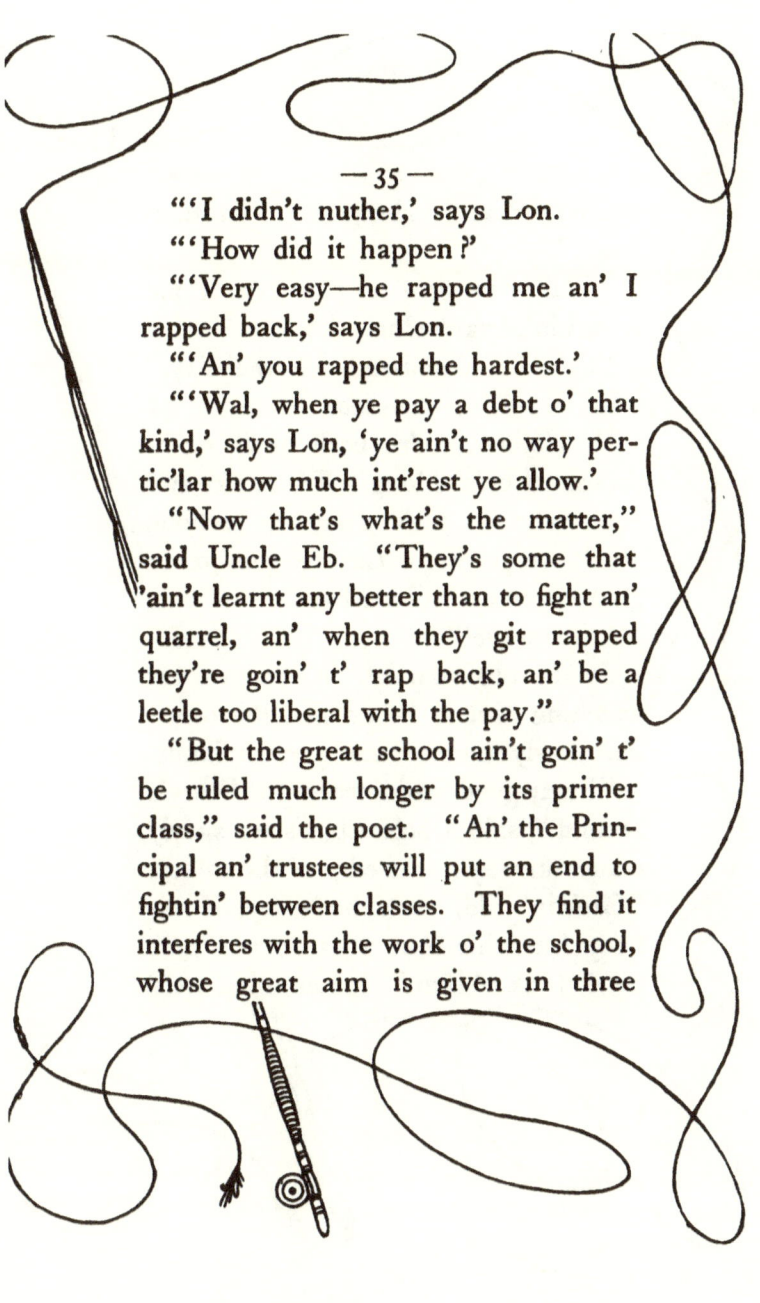

"'I didn't nuther,' says Lon.

"'How did it happen ?'

"'Very easy—he rapped me an' I rapped back,' says Lon.

"'An' you rapped the hardest.'

"'Wal, when ye pay a debt o' that kind,' says Lon, 'ye ain't no way per-tic'lar how much int'rest ye allow.'

"Now that's what's the matter," said Uncle Eb. "They's some that 'ain't learnt any better than to fight an' quarrel, an' when they git rapped they're goin' t' rap back, an' be a leetle too liberal with the pay."

"But the great school ain't goin' t' be ruled much longer by its primer class," said the poet. "An' the Prin-cipal an' trustees will put an end to fightin' between classes. They find it interferes with the work o' the school, whose great aim is given in three

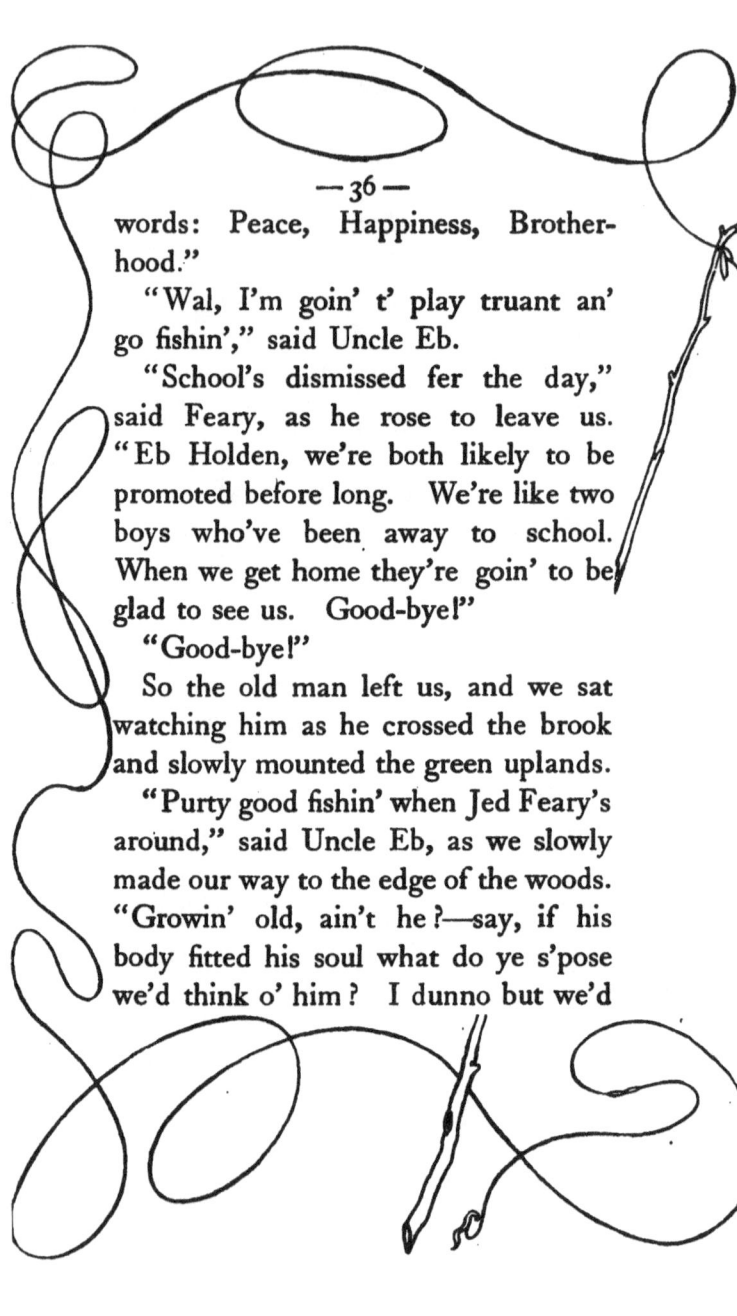

words: Peace, Happiness, Brother-
hood."

"Wal, I'm goin' t' play truant an'
go fishin'," said Uncle Eb.

"School's dismissed fer the day,"
said Feary, as he rose to leave us.
"Eb Holden, we're both likely to be
promoted before long. We're like two
boys who've been away to school.
When we get home they're goin' to be
glad to see us. Good-bye!"

"Good-bye!"

So the old man left us, and we sat
watching him as he crossed the brook
and slowly mounted the green uplands.

"Purty good fishin' when Jed Feary's
around," said Uncle Eb, as we slowly
made our way to the edge of the woods.
"Growin' old, ain't he?—say, if his
body fitted his soul what do ye s'pose
we'd think o' him? I dunno but we'd

feel like gittin' on our knees when he
come around. It wouldn't do. This
world's no place fer angels, after all.
Wal, come on, le's quit thinkin' an'
have some fun."

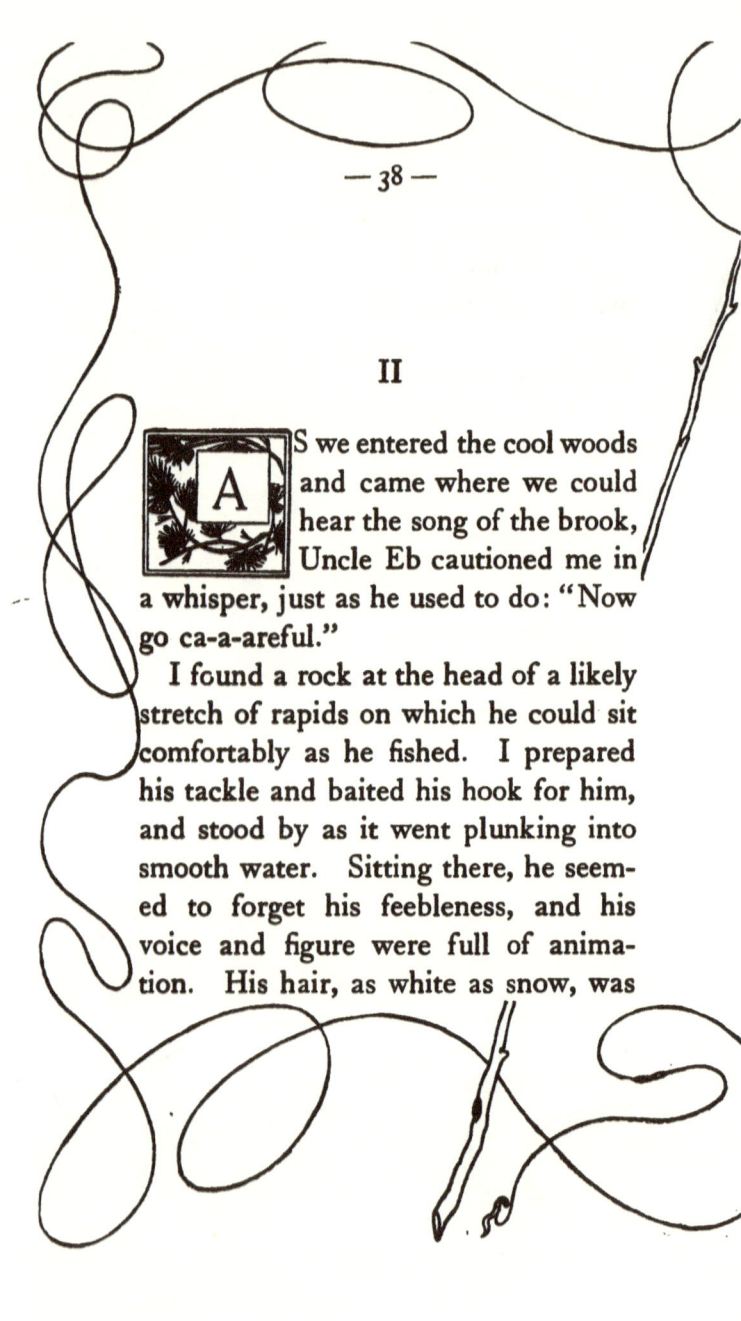

II

AS we entered the cool woods and came where we could hear the song of the brook, Uncle Eb cautioned me in a whisper, just as he used to do: "Now go ca-a-areful."

I found a rock at the head of a likely stretch of rapids on which he could sit comfortably as he fished. I prepared his tackle and baited his hook for him, and stood by as it went plunking into smooth water. Sitting there, he seemed to forget his feebleness, and his voice and figure were full of anima-tion. His hair, as white as snow, was like the crown of glory of which David sings.

He kept hauling and giving out. Now and then, as he felt a nibble, he addressed the fish:

"How d' do? Come ag'in," he said, as he continued to work his line. "Tut, tut! you're another!" he exclaimed, with a sharp twitch.

The trout was a large one, and Uncle Eb, with a six-ounce rod, had not been able to lift and swing him ashore in the old fashion. He held on with jiggling hands and a look of great animation as the fish took line in half a dozen quick rushes.

"You're tryin' to jerk me out o' my boots"—the words were emphasized and broken here and there by the struggle. The rod's vibration had got into his voice and all the upper part

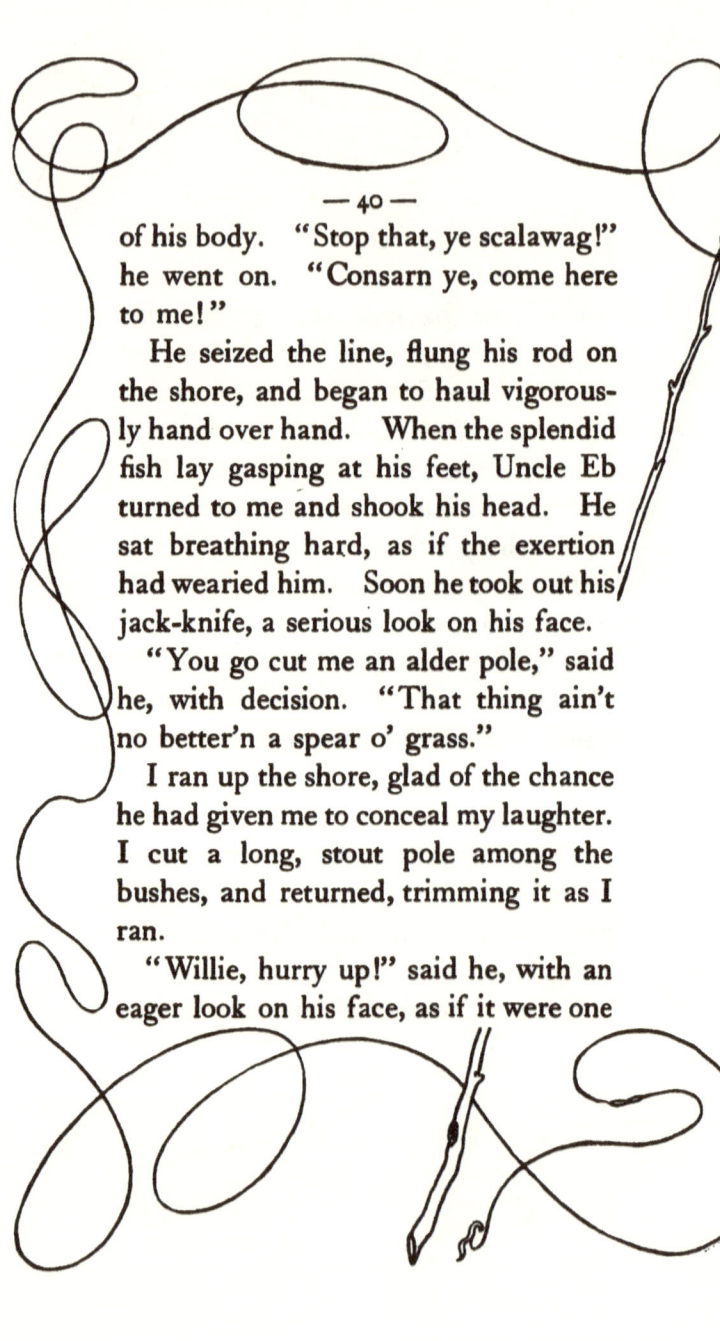

of his body. "Stop that, ye scalawag!"
he went on. "Consarn ye, come here
to me!"

He seized the line, flung his rod on
the shore, and began to haul vigorous-
ly hand over hand. When the splendid
fish lay gasping at his feet, Uncle Eb
turned to me and shook his head. He
sat breathing hard, as if the exertion
had wearied him. Soon he took out his
jack-knife, a serious look on his face.

"You go cut me an alder pole," said
he, with decision. "That thing ain't
no better'n a spear o' grass."

I ran up the shore, glad of the chance
he had given me to conceal my laughter.
I cut a long, stout pole among the
bushes, and returned, trimming it as I
ran.

"Willie, hurry up!" said he, with an
eager look on his face, as if it were one

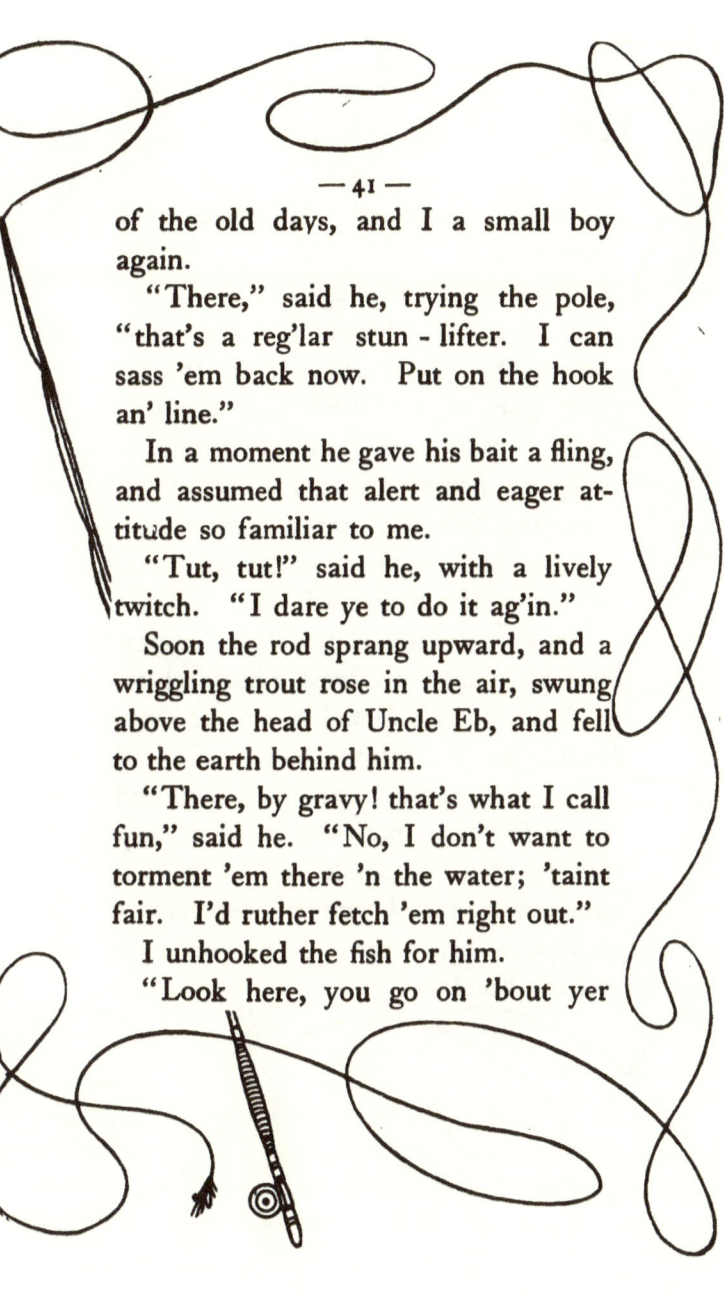

of the old days, and I a small boy again.

"There," said he, trying the pole, "that's a reg'lar stun - lifter. I can sass 'em back now. Put on the hook an' line."

In a moment he gave his bait a fling, and assumed that alert and eager attitude so familiar to me.

"Tut, tut!" said he, with a lively twitch. "I dare ye to do it ag'in."

Soon the rod sprang upward, and a wriggling trout rose in the air, swung above the head of Uncle Eb, and fell to the earth behind him.

"There, by gravy! that's what I call fun," said he. "No, I don't want to torment 'em there 'n the water; 'taint fair. I'd ruther fetch 'em right out."

I unhooked the fish for him.

"Look here, you go on 'bout yer

business," he added. "I can bait my own hook."

I left him and began to whip my way down the brook. It was good fishing, but the scene was by far the best part of it. What was there in those lovely and familiar shores to keep my heart so busy? The crows, hurrying like boys let out of school, seemed to denounce me as an alien. A crane flew over my head, crunkling a fierce complaint of me, and the startled kingfisher was most inhospitable.

A small, bare-footed boy passed me, fishing on the farther bank. He had a happy face, and mine—well, I turned away for very shame of it. The boy looked at me critically, as if I were a trespasser, and I remembered how I felt years ago, when I saw a stranger on the brook.

I remembered how, as a boy, I used to long for a watch-chain, and how once Uncle Eb hung his upon my coat, and said I could "call it mine." So it goes all through life. We are the veriest children, and there is nothing one may really own. He may call it his for a little while, just to satisfy him. The whole matter of deeds and titles had become now a kind of baby's play. You may think you own the land, and you pass on; but there it is, while others, full of the same old illusion, take your place.

I followed the brook to where it idled on, bordered with buttercups, in a great meadow. The music and the color halted me, and I lay on my back in the tall grass for a little while, and looked up at the sky and listened. There under the clover tops I could

hear the low, sweet music of many
wings—the continuous treble of the
honey-bee in chord with flashes of
deep bass from the wings of that big,
wild, improvident cousin of his.

Above this lower heaven I could
hear a tournament of bobolinks. They
flew over me, and clung in the grass
tops and sang—their notes bursting
out like those of a plucked string.
What a pressure of delight was behind
them! Hope and I used to go there
for berries when we were children, and
later—when youth had come, and the
colors of the wild rose and the tiger-
lily were in our faces—we found a
secret joy in being alone together.
Those days there was something beautiful in that hidden fear we had of each
other—was it not the native, imperial
majesty of innocence? The look of

her eyes seemed to lift me up and pre-
pare me for any sacrifice. That or-
chestra of the meadow spoke our
thoughts for us—youth, delight and
love were in its music.

Soon I heard a merry laugh and the
sound of feet approaching, and then
the voice of a young man.

"Mary, I love you," it said, "and I
would die for your sake."

The same old story, and I knew that
he meant every word of it. What
Mary may have said to him I know
well enough, too, although it came not
to my ears; for when I rose, by and by,
and crossed the woodland and saw
them walking up the slopes, she all
in white and crowned with meadow
flowers, I observed that his arm supported her in the right way.

I took down my rod and hurried up

4

stream, and came soon where I could see Uncle Eb sitting motionless and leaning on a tree trunk. I approached him silently. His head leaned forward; the "pole" lay upon his knees. Like a child, weary of play, he had fallen asleep. His trout lay in a row beside him; there were at least a dozen. That old body was now, indeed, a very bad fit, and more—it was too shabby for a spirit so noble and brave. I knew, as I looked down upon him, that Uncle Eb would fish no more after that day. In a moment there came a twitch on the line. He woke suddenly, tightened his grasp, and flung another fish into the air. It broke free and fell upon the ripples.

"Huh! ketched me nappin'," said he. "I declare, Bill, I'm kind o' shamed."

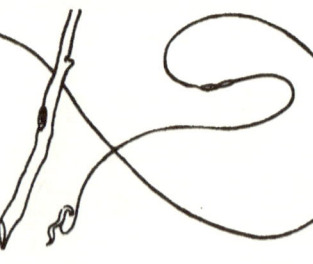

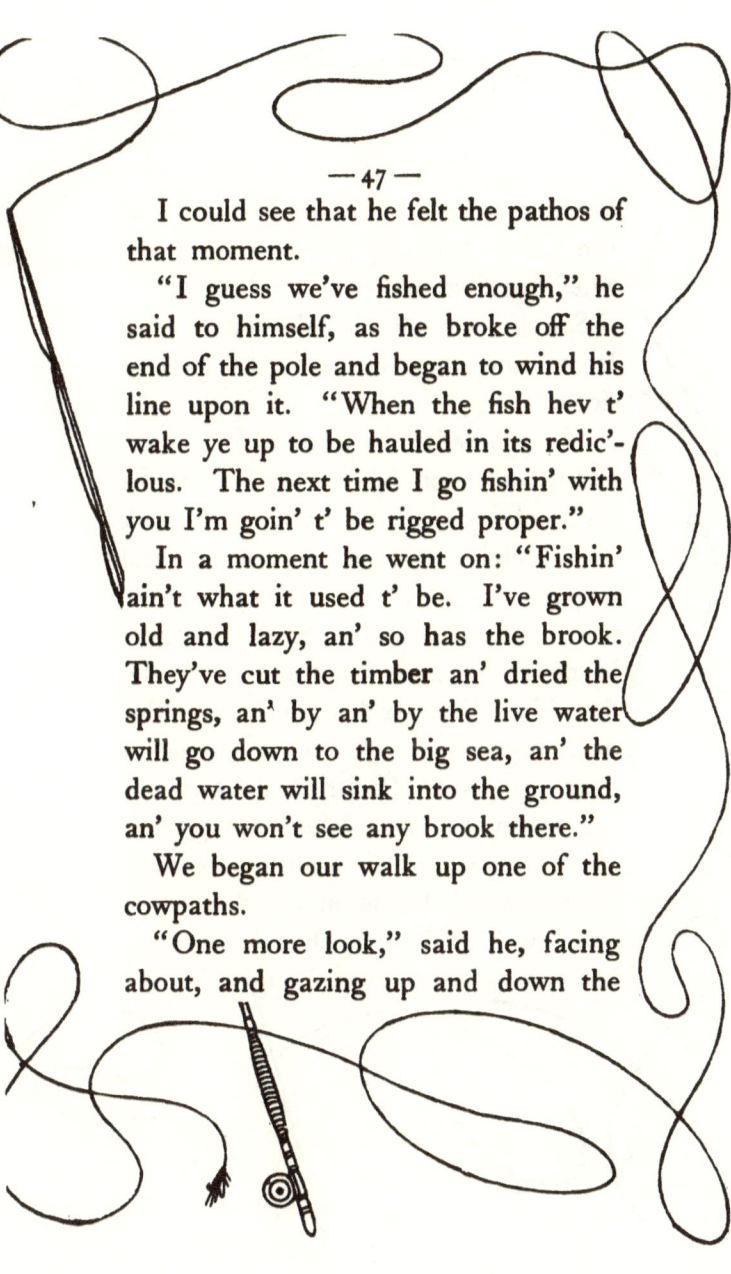

I could see that he felt the pathos of that moment.

"I guess we've fished enough," he said to himself, as he broke off the end of the pole and began to wind his line upon it. "When the fish hev t' wake ye up to be hauled in its redic'-lous. The next time I go fishin' with you I'm goin' t' be rigged proper."

In a moment he went on: "Fishin' ain't what it used t' be. I've grown old and lazy, an' so has the brook. They've cut the timber an' dried the springs, an' by an' by the live water will go down to the big sea, an' the dead water will sink into the ground, an' you won't see any brook there."

We began our walk up one of the cowpaths.

"One more look," said he, facing about, and gazing up and down the familiar valley. "We've had a lot o' fun here—'bout as much as we're entitled to, I guess—let 'em have it."

So, in a way, he deeded Tinkle Brook and its valley to future generations.

We proceeded in silence for a moment, and soon he added: "That little brook has done a lot fer us. It took our thoughts off the hard work, and helped us fergit the mortgage, an' taught us to laugh like the rapid water. It never owed us anything after the day Mose Tupper lost his pole. Put it all together, I guess I've laughed a year over that. 'Bout the best payin' job we ever done. Mose thought he had a whale, an' I don't blame him. Fact is, a lost fish is an awful liar. A trout would deceive the devil when he's way down out o' sight in the water, an' his weight is telegraphed through twenty feet o' line. When ye fetch him up an' look him square in the eye he tells a different story. I blame the fish more'n I do the folks.

"That 'swallered pole' was a kind of a magic wand round here in Faraway. Ye could allwus fetch a laugh with it. Sometimes I think they must 'a' lost one commandment, an' that is: Be happy. Ye can't be happy an' be bad. I never see a bad man in my life that was hevin' fun. Let me hear a man laugh an' I'll tell ye what kind o' metal there is in him. There ain't any sech devilish sound in the world as the laugh of a wicked man. It's like the cry o' the swift, an' you 'member what that was."

Uncle Eb shook with laughter as I

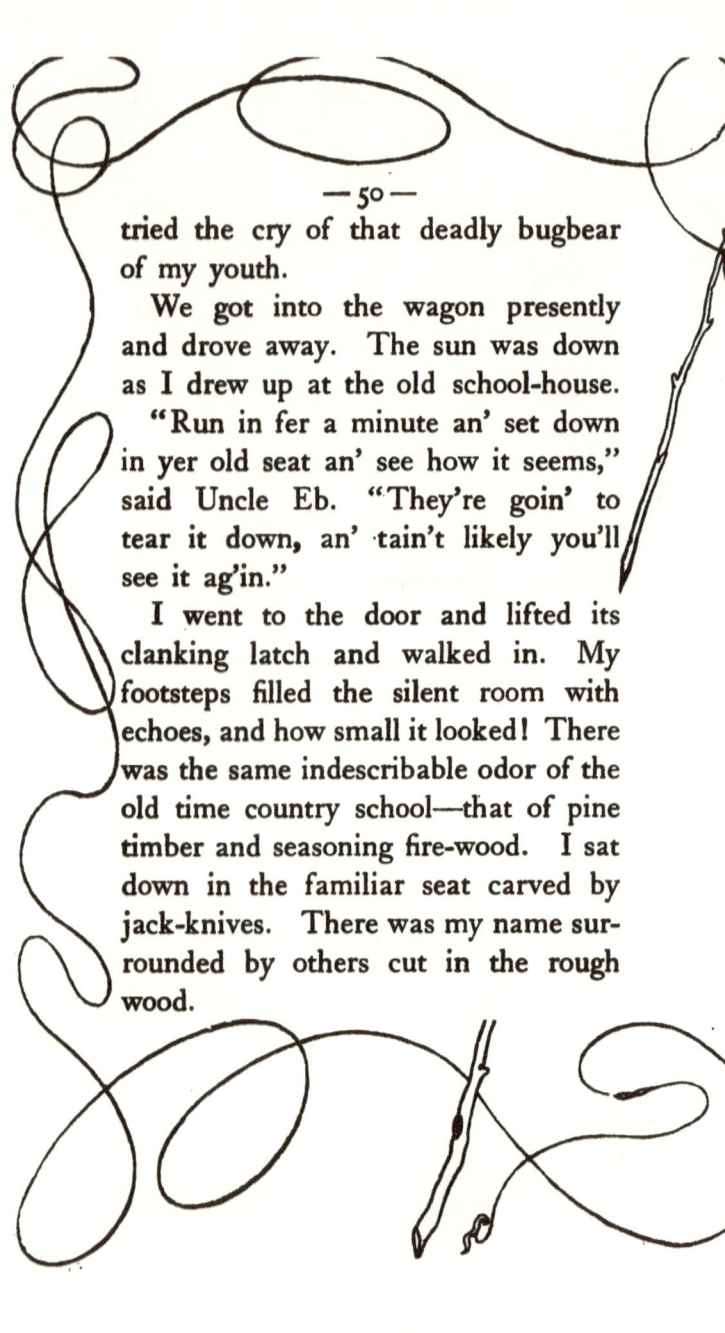

tried the cry of that deadly bugbear
of my youth.

We got into the wagon presently
and drove away. The sun was down
as I drew up at the old school-house.

"Run in fer a minute an' set down
in yer old seat an' see how it seems,"
said Uncle Eb. "They're goin' to
tear it down, an' tain't likely you'll
see it ag'in."

I went to the door and lifted its
clanking latch and walked in. My
footsteps filled the silent room with
echoes, and how small it looked! There
was the same indescribable odor of the
old time country school—that of pine
timber and seasoning fire-wood. I sat
down in the familiar seat carved by
jack-knives. There was my name sur-
rounded by others cut in the rough
wood.

Ghosts began to file into the dusky room, and above a plaintive hum of insects it seemed as if I could hear the voices of children and bits of the old lessons — that loud, triumphant sound of tender intelligence as it began to seize the alphabet; those parrot - like answers: "Round like a ball," "Three - fourths water and one - fourth land," and others like them.

"William Brower, stop whispering!" I seemed to hear the teacher say. What was the writing on the black-board? I rose and walked to it as I had been wont to do when the teacher gave his command. There in the silence of the closing day I learned my last lesson in the old school-house. These lines in the large, familiar script of Feary, who it seems had been a

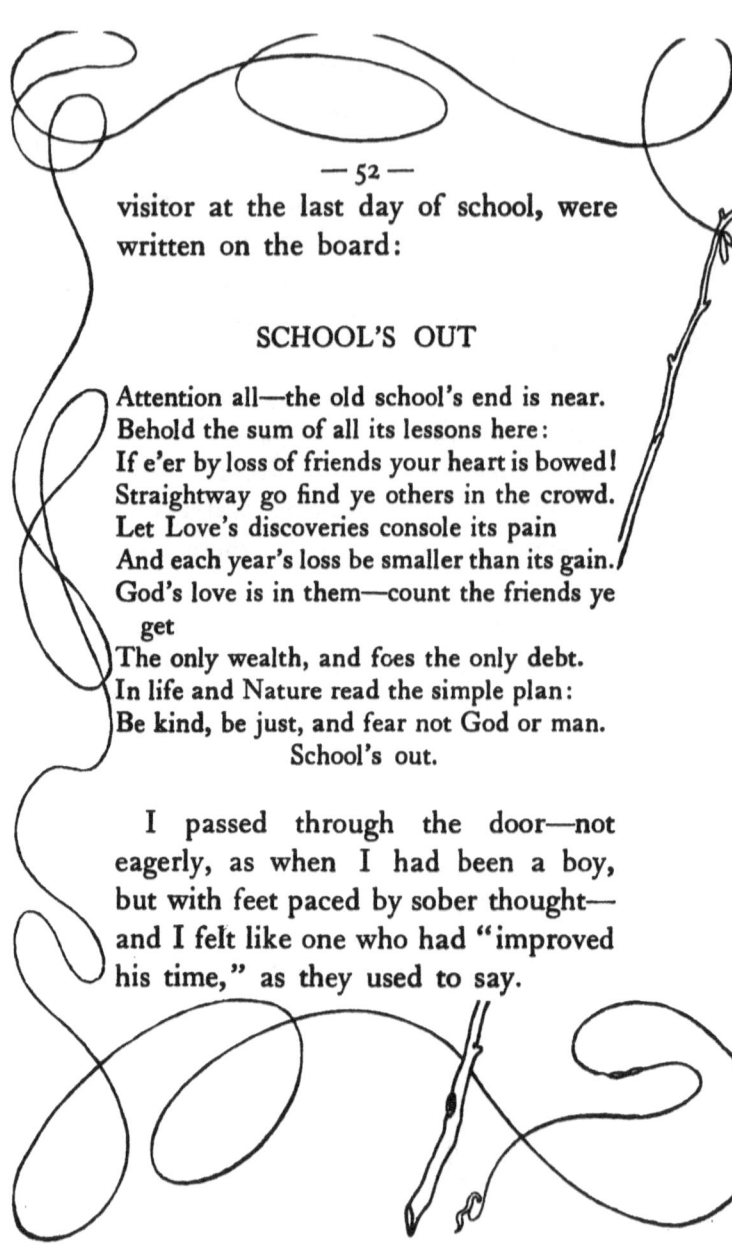

visitor at the last day of school, were
written on the board:

SCHOOL'S OUT

Attention all—the old school's end is near.
Behold the sum of all its lessons here:
If e'er by loss of friends your heart is bowed!
Straightway go find ye others in the crowd.
Let Love's discoveries console its pain
And each year's loss be smaller than its gain.
God's love is in them—count the friends ye
  get
The only wealth, and foes the only debt.
In life and Nature read the simple plan:
Be kind, be just, and fear not God or man.
          School's out.

I passed through the door—not
eagerly, as when I had been a boy,
but with feet paced by sober thought—
and I felt like one who had "improved
his time," as they used to say.

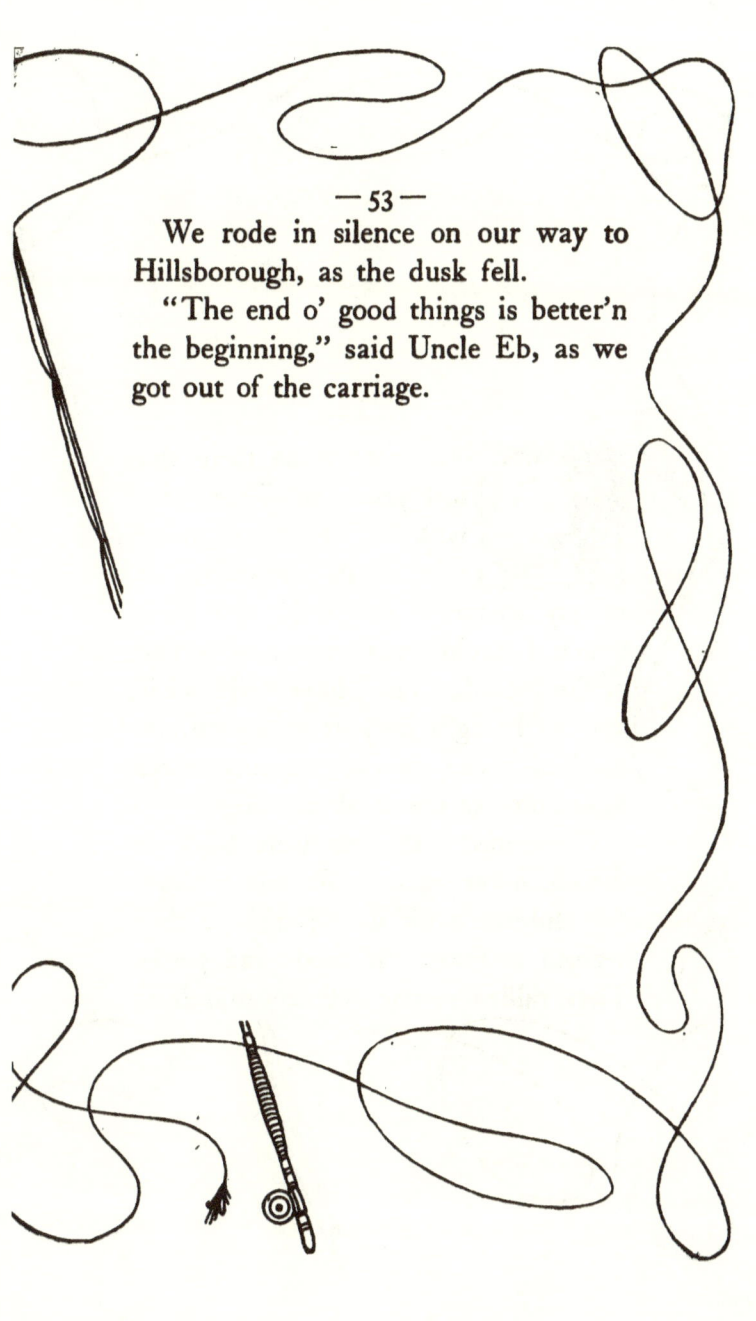

We rode in silence on our way to Hillsborough, as the dusk fell.

"The end o' good things is better'n the beginning," said Uncle Eb, as we got out of the carriage.

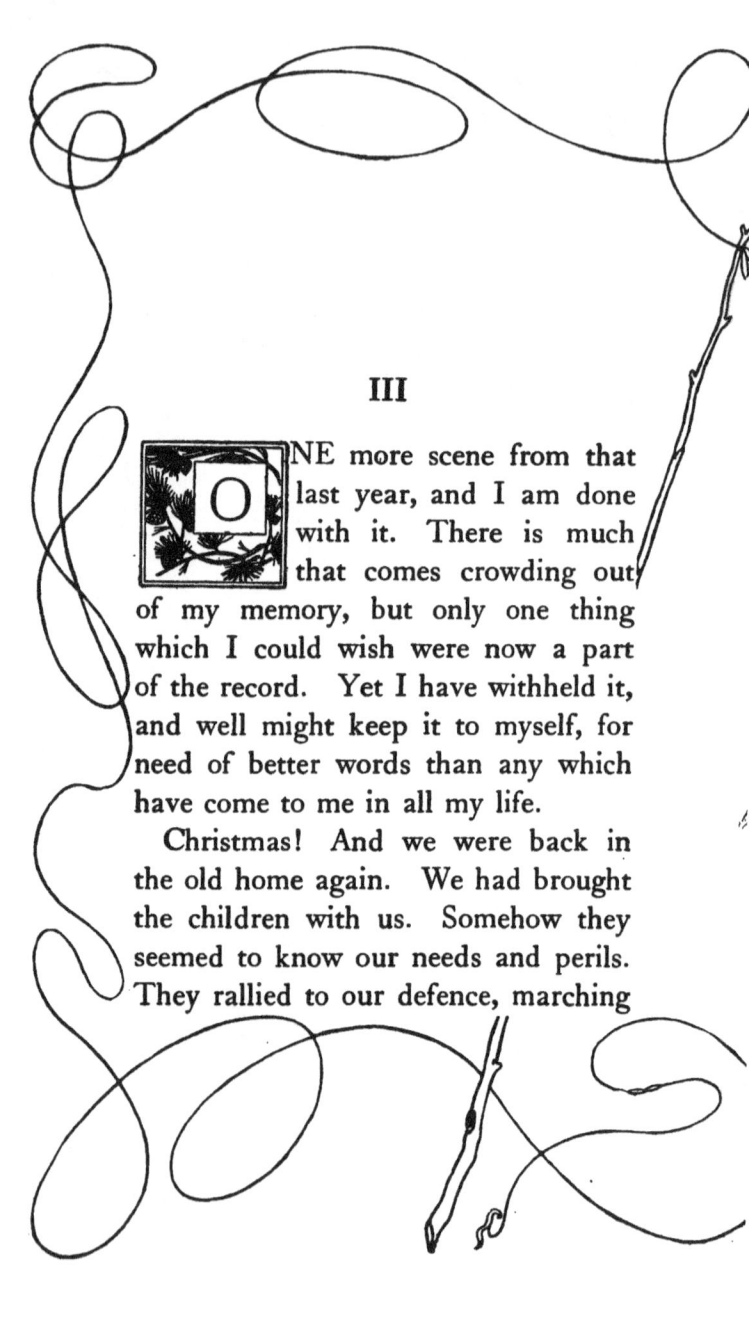

III

ONE more scene from that last year, and I am done with it. There is much that comes crowding out of my memory, but only one thing which I could wish were now a part of the record. Yet I have withheld it, and well might keep it to myself, for need of better words than any which have come to me in all my life.

Christmas! And we were back in the old home again. We had brought the children with us. Somehow they seemed to know our needs and perils. They rallied to our defence, marching

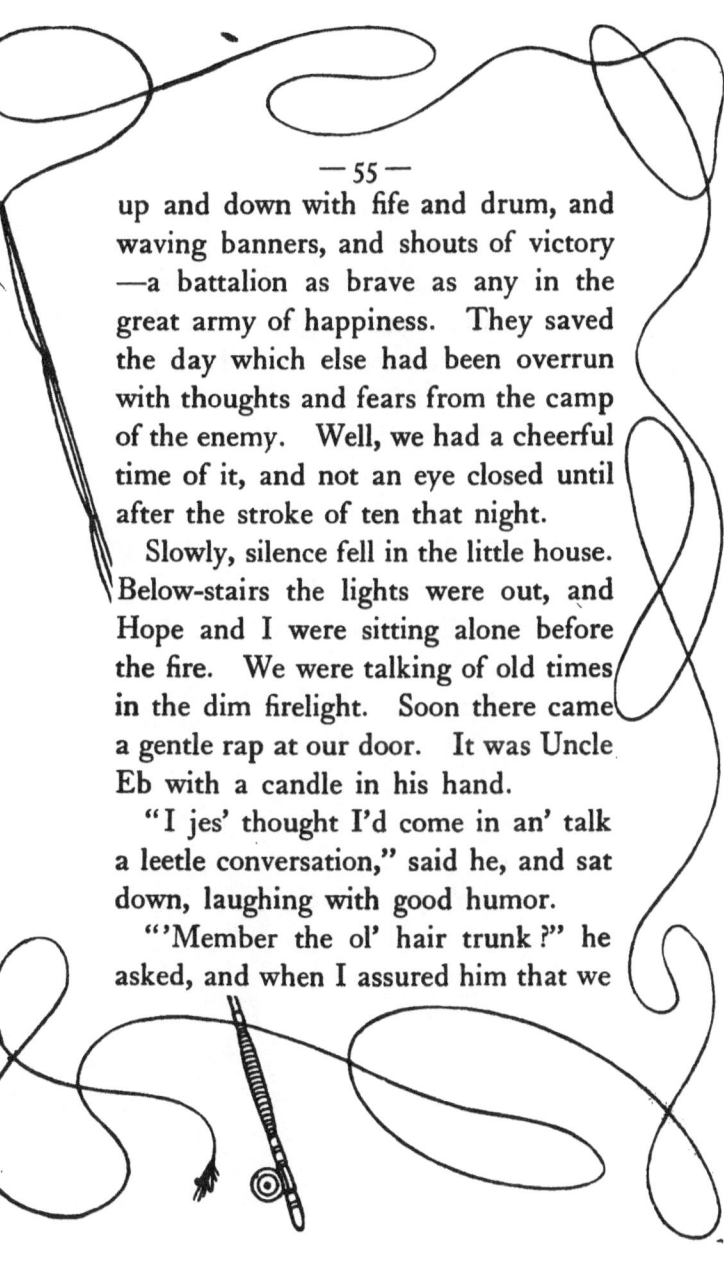

up and down with fife and drum, and
waving banners, and shouts of victory
—a battalion as brave as any in the
great army of happiness. They saved
the day which else had been overrun
with thoughts and fears from the camp
of the enemy. Well, we had a cheerful
time of it, and not an eye closed until
after the stroke of ten that night.

Slowly, silence fell in the little house.
Below-stairs the lights were out, and
Hope and I were sitting alone before
the fire. We were talking of old times
in the dim firelight. Soon there came
a gentle rap at our door. It was Uncle
Eb with a candle in his hand.

"I jes' thought I'd come in an' talk
a leetle conversation," said he, and sat
down, laughing with good humor.

"'Member the ol' hair trunk?" he
asked, and when I assured him that we

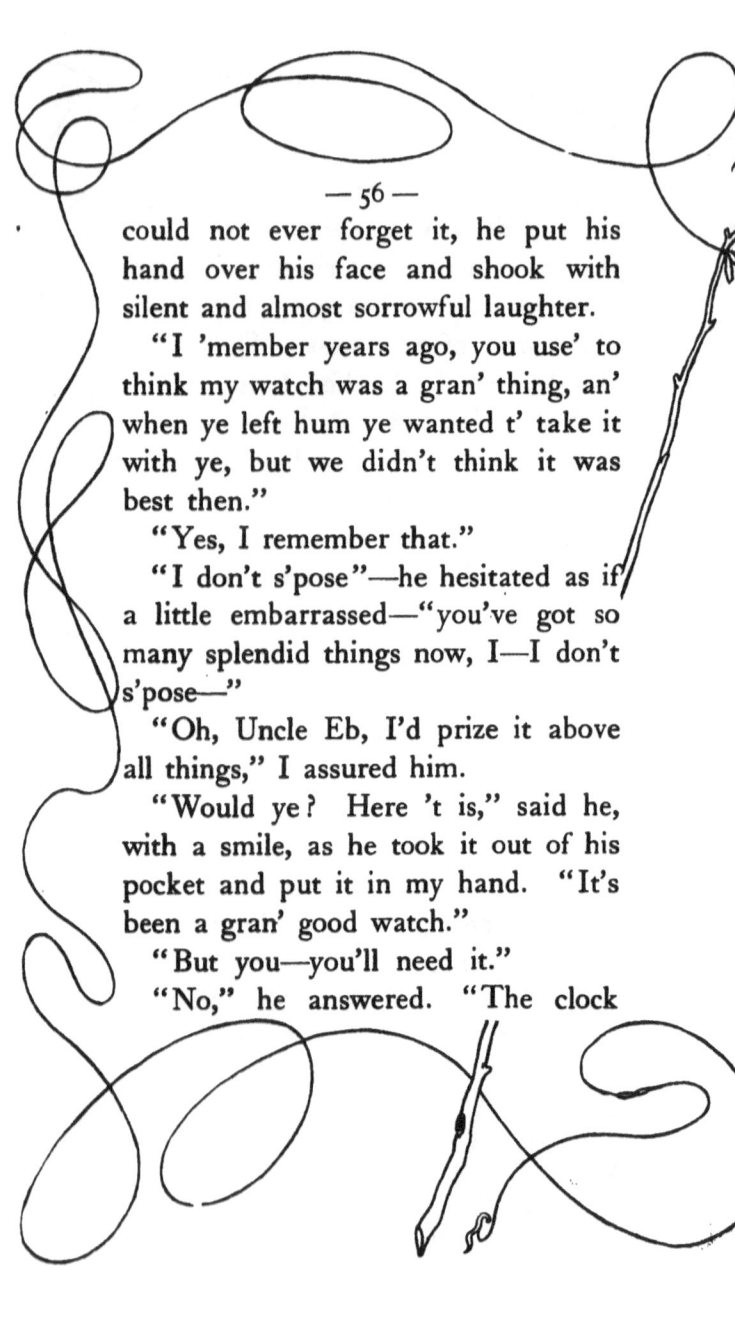

could not ever forget it, he put his hand over his face and shook with silent and almost sorrowful laughter.

"I 'member years ago, you use' to think my watch was a gran' thing, an' when ye left hum ye wanted t' take it with ye, but we didn't think it was best then."

"Yes, I remember that."

"I don't s'pose"—he hesitated as if a little embarrassed—"you've got so many splendid things now, I—I don't s'pose—"

"Oh, Uncle Eb, I'd prize it above all things," I assured him.

"Would ye? Here 't is," said he, with a smile, as he took it out of his pocket and put it in my hand. "It's been a gran' good watch."

"But you—you'll need it."

"No," he answered. "The clock

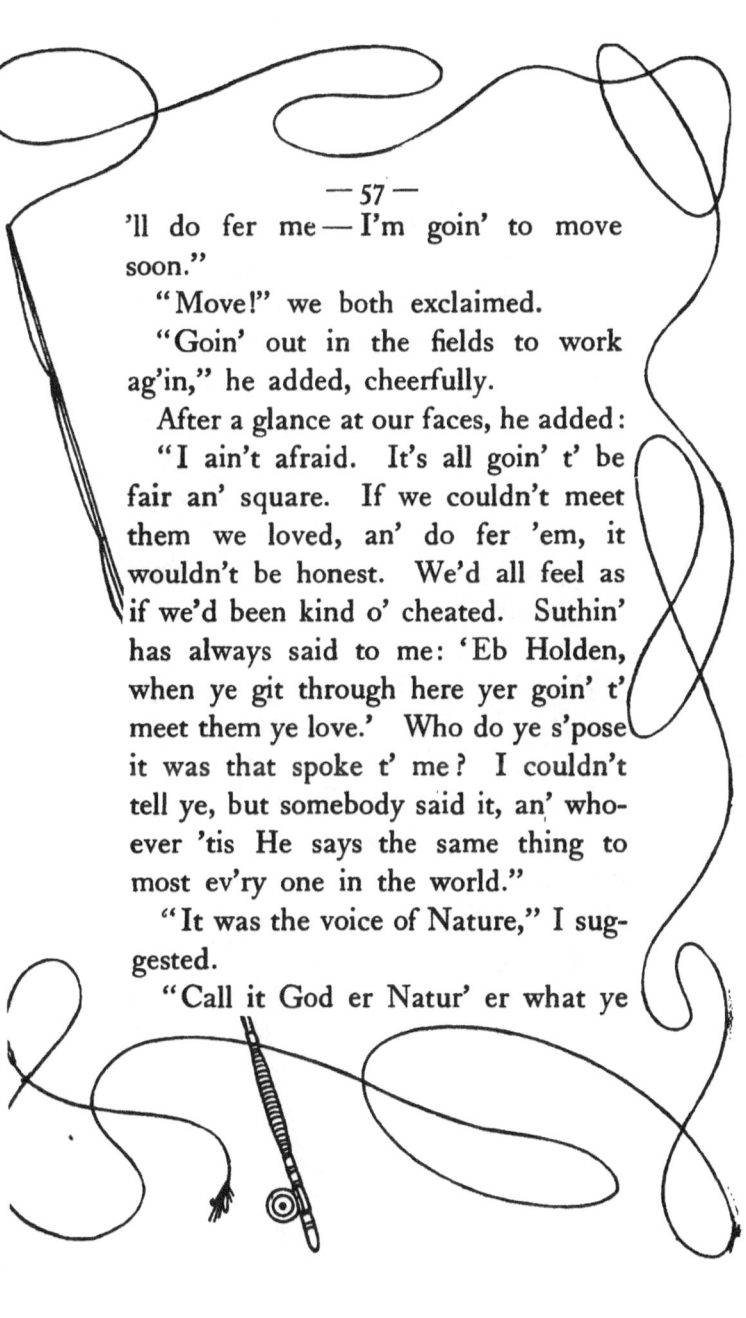

'll do fer me — I'm goin' to move soon."

"Move!" we both exclaimed.

"Goin' out in the fields to work ag'in," he added, cheerfully.

After a glance at our faces, he added:

"I ain't afraid. It's all goin' t' be fair an' square. If we couldn't meet them we loved, an' do fer 'em, it wouldn't be honest. We'd all feel as if we'd been kind o' cheated. Suthin' has always said to me: 'Eb Holden, when ye git through here yer goin' t' meet them ye love.' Who do ye s'pose it was that spoke t' me? I couldn't tell ye, but somebody said it, an' who-ever 'tis He says the same thing to most ev'ry one in the world."

"It was the voice of Nature," I suggested.

"Call it God er Natur' er what ye

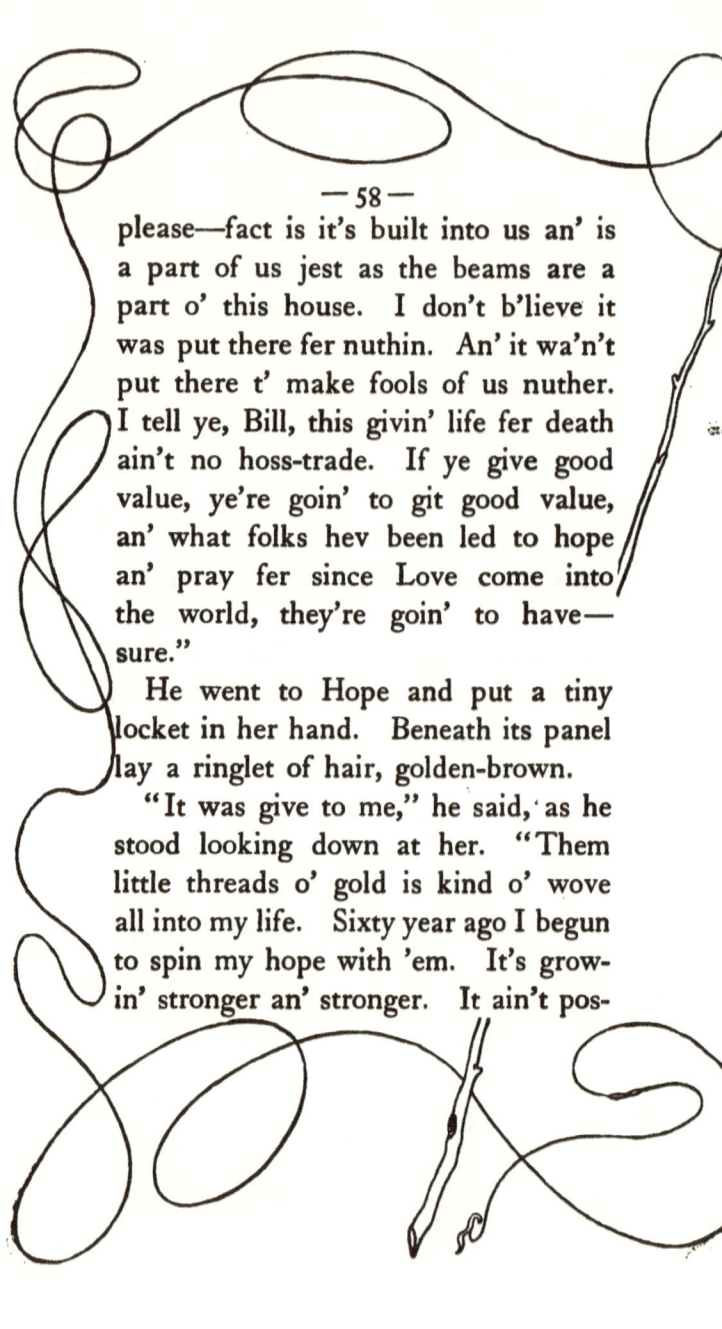

please—fact is it's built into us an' is a part of us jest as the beams are a part o' this house. I don't b'lieve it was put there fer nuthin. An' it wa'n't put there t' make fools of us nuther. I tell ye, Bill, this givin' life fer death ain't no hoss-trade. If ye give good value, ye're goin' to git good value, an' what folks hev been led to hope an' pray fer since Love come into the world, they're goin' to have— sure."

He went to Hope and put a tiny locket in her hand. Beneath its panel lay a ringlet of hair, golden-brown.

"It was give to me," he said, as he stood looking down at her. "Them little threads o' gold is kind o' wove all into my life. Sixty year ago I begun to spin my hope with 'em. It's growin' stronger an' stronger. It ain't pos-

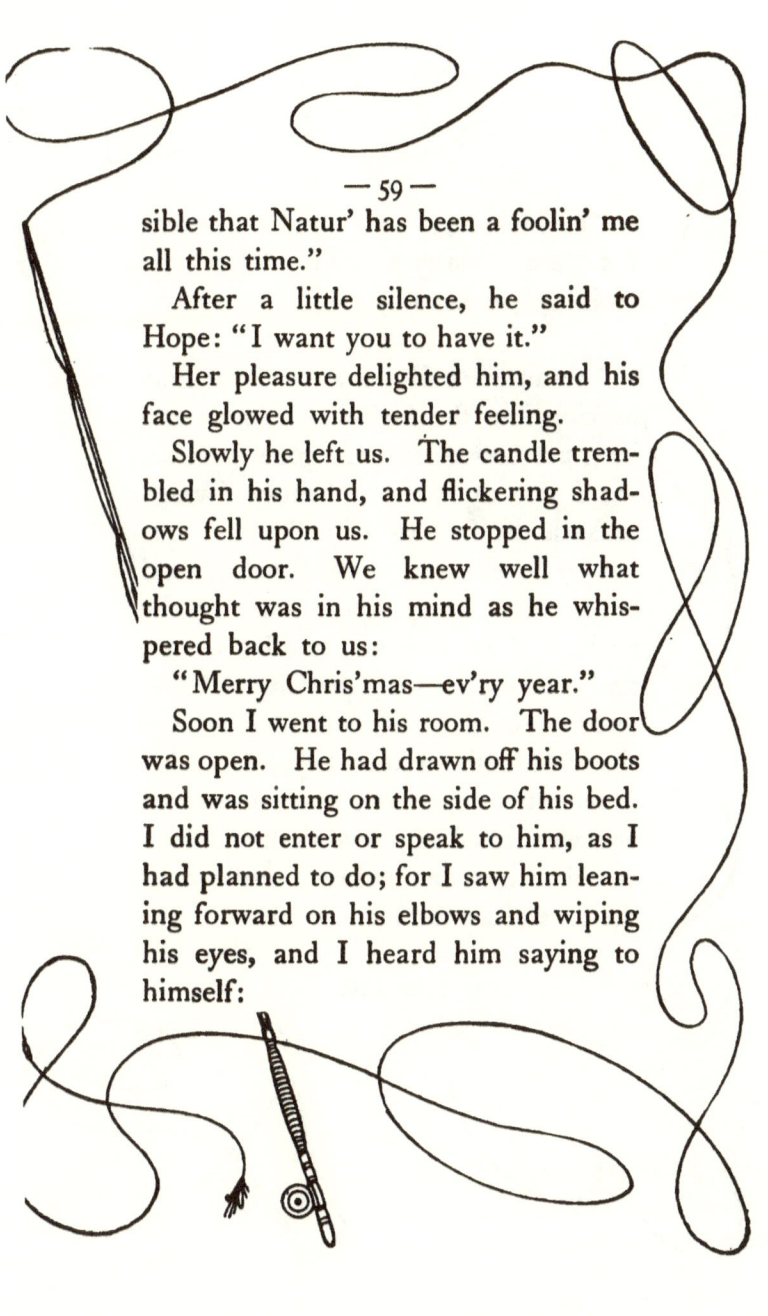

sible that Natur' has been a foolin' me all this time."

After a little silence, he said to Hope: "I want you to have it."

Her pleasure delighted him, and his face glowed with tender feeling.

Slowly he left us. The candle trembled in his hand, and flickering shadows fell upon us. He stopped in the open door. We knew well what thought was in his mind as he whispered back to us:

"Merry Chris'mas—ev'ry year."

Soon I went to his room. The door was open. He had drawn off his boots and was sitting on the side of his bed. I did not enter or speak to him, as I had planned to do; for I saw him leaning forward on his elbows and wiping his eyes, and I heard him saying to himself:

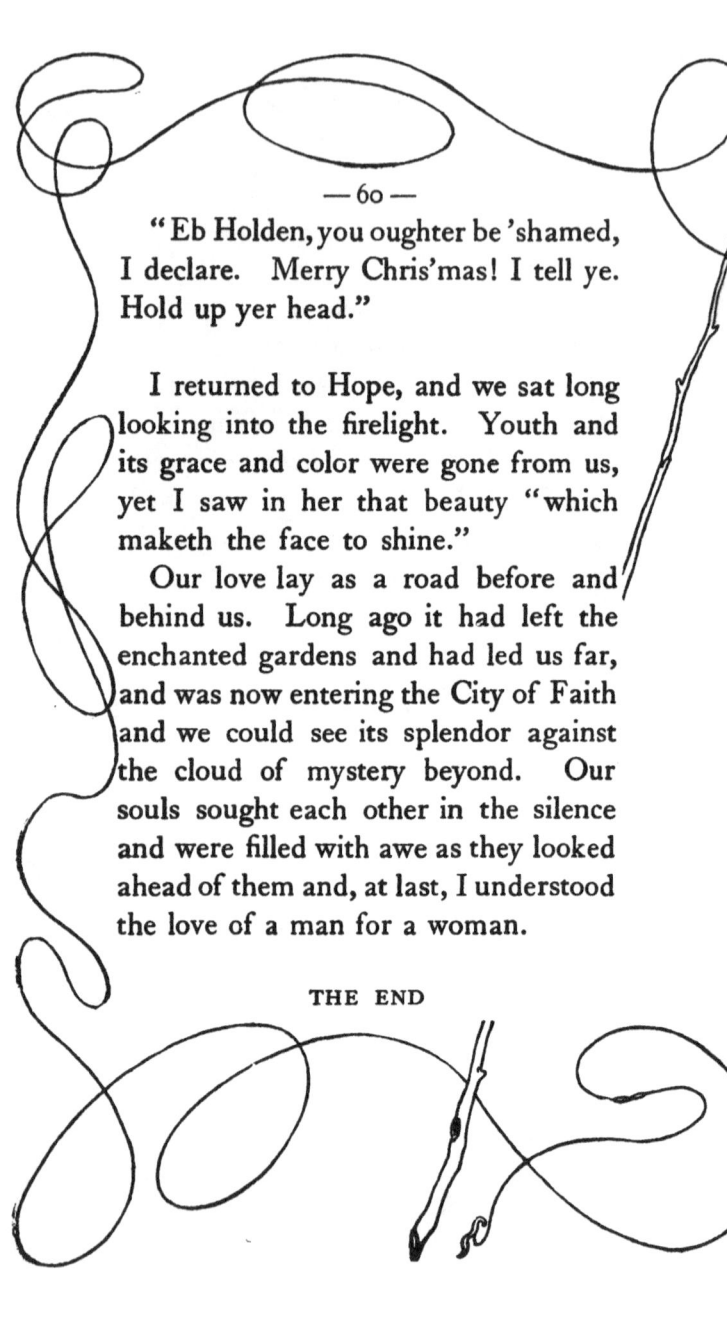

"Eb Holden, you oughter be 'shamed,
I declare. Merry Chris'mas! I tell ye.
Hold up yer head."

I returned to Hope, and we sat long
looking into the firelight. Youth and
its grace and color were gone from us,
yet I saw in her that beauty "which
maketh the face to shine."

Our love lay as a road before and
behind us. Long ago it had left the
enchanted gardens and had led us far,
and was now entering the City of Faith
and we could see its splendor against
the cloud of mystery beyond. Our
souls sought each other in the silence
and were filled with awe as they looked
ahead of them and, at last, I understood
the love of a man for a woman.

THE END

www.ingramcontent.com/pod-product-compliance
Lightning Source LLC
Chambersburg PA
CBHW021938170626
46807CB00007B/3167